ALWAYS YOU

NOT MY FIRST RODEO

MISSY BEST

ALWAYS YOU

By Missy Best

A cowboy dream.
  Want, need, can't have.

#1 NOT MY FIRST RODEO SERIES

Published in Australia, 22–05–25

978-0-9872355-9-6 (paperback)
B0DTWQB7NZ (ASIN ebook Amazon)

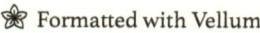 Formatted with Vellum

DEDICATION

For my real cowboy, whose favourite colour is orange and favourite person is me.

And for all the women, and men, who know what it's like to be told *anything for you, babe.*

ABOUT THE AUTHOR

I'm an established Australian author, and after absorbing myself in reading and writing crime fiction during my career, I have had a change of heart.

While writing my latest crime novel my characters kept dragging me more explicitly into their personal lives. It ended up feeling like a clash of genres that didn't quite fit, and I started researching the romance/romantsy/spicy romance/smut genre. It has come a very long way since *50 Shades of Grey*, and I am more than comfortable wearing this new hat.

I remember my Nan having a stash of Mills and Boons books under her bed, the ones with the half-naked couples on the front, and thought of her often while writing this book.

I believe we all need some escapism and romance, regardless of our age or what we do in our daily lives. I've thoroughly enjoyed a break from the deep dark places my crime novels take me, and I hope my new readers do too.

Missy B x

ALWAYS YOU

I'm a country girl happy to live my smalltown life until I meet my first real cowboy in the flesh.
He's off limits though.
Or is he?
After an unexpected encounter followed by a crushing rejection, I swear off cowboys and move on.
While happily caught up in wedding plans, I keep crossing paths with my dream cowboy and am left to wonder, *why do we always want what we can't have?*

CONTENT

This book contains adult themes and sex scenes between consenting adults. This novel is set in Australia in the early 2000s and aims to be as true as possible to the language, technology, culture, music and lifestyle of that time.

This was before TikTok, Instagram, Facebook, Google and mobile phones distracted and dominated our lives, when people phoned on the landline and long-distance lovers poured their hearts and souls into handwritten letters.

It is set in real places in Australia and inspired by the culture of small towns and Australian cowboys of that time who knew what they wanted even when they didn't have the words.

1

SKYE

I watch from the shed door as Beth disappears in a cloud of dust. Quinton, his Akubra pulled down low, stands in the driveway for the longest time, one arm on the head of his favourite Kelpie, the other reaching up occasionally to wipe his eyes.

I watch his shaking shoulders, desperate to run out, wrap my arms around his waist, disappear into his chest, snuggle my head into that space next to his heart, and comfort him.

Reluctantly I return to work, doing my best to be as efficient and impressive as possible as I muck out the pig pens.

Our small team at this Australian piggery works comfortably around each other. Quinton, my new boss, French couple Monty and Adeline who speak in endearingly halted English, myself and Austin, whose parents started the piggery with just thirty sows two decades ago. Austin is like the big brother I never had, complete with the arm-punching, teasing and hair ruffling.

The piggery has grown to almost five hundred sows, and sits on the flats of a large property that's a mix of green, rolling hills and pasture paddocks not far from my hometown of Scone, Australia. A historic town north of Sydney, Scone is described in tourism brochures as the *Horse Capital of Australia*. Population, five thousand, plus the surrounding farming community which recently welcomed a new hard-working, enterprising couple, Quinton and Beth.

Quinton, originally from a cattle station in central Queensland, and Beth, a lawyer in Sydney, bought the farm to fulfill Quinton's dream to strike out on his own and try something completely new in agriculture.

A keen horseman and a now-retired amateur rodeo rider, he fell in love with the rolling hills and lush landscape of Scone when he competed on the rodeo circuit in the nineties. He saw it as the land of opportunity, and with his long-time girlfriend Beth's backing and his share of their family farm after his brother bought him out, they invested in this thriving, growing farm business which supplies pork to the most exclusive city restaurants around the country.

Time passes quickly with casual conversation and a few laughs along the way. Quinton is distracted, but nobody seems to notice.

I notice.

I've noticed a lot lately. Long absences by Beth, who doesn't seem as invested in living out their farming dream as Quinton. Also, a stark difference in the way Quinton and Beth are around each other. When they first arrived, they were affectionate and always holding hands, standing close to each other, eager to learn the ropes, excited and enthusiastic.

Now they are strained. No touching, very little talking and *all business*.

I put it down to the stress of Beth's job as a hot shot young corporate lawyer, with long hours and endless travel between here and Sydney.

In my view, Beth doesn't deserve Quinton; she seems more interested in her city job than her strikingly handsome, strong, silent-type who stands at the gate with tears in his eyes every time she drives away.

Cowboys cry too.

Quinton and Austin spend their lunch break talking animatedly about their plans to reduce the environmental impacts of the piggery where I've worked for six years, since I was sixteen. I hang off every word, as it's the most I ever hear Quinton speak. He's a lot more reserved around the rest of us. When it comes to conversation, *less is more*.

Quinton has notebooks filled with new and innovative ideas. I overheard him tell Austin he'd completed a Nuffield scholarship about holistic farming for cattle a couple of years ago, but isn't jumping into things too quickly. He wants to make sure he has his head around how to apply his ideas to pigs before he takes big risks. Especially given it is his and Beth's business, not just his.

Beth. I can't say I dislike her. She's hard not to like. If I wasn't so obsessed with her boyfriend and jealous that she met this perfect cowboy before I did, we could probably be friends. She's smart and funny, and as comfortable in the pig sheds covered in muck as the Supreme Court in a white shirt, pin-striped suit and high heels.

Monty and Adeline leave early, Austin as well, so it is just Quinton and I left to pack up. Make that, just I. Quinton disappeared before I could say goodbye. Maybe to drown his sorrows. When Beth left today, it seemed so final, as though the short, sharp words they'd been snapping at each other lately had run out for good.

The sheds are silent, apart from the comforting sounds of the pigs settling down for the night. I love this place. It is like my second home.

I step out of the shower, singing to myself as I dry off and get dressed. I look in the small mirror above the sink and smile at the girl looking back at me. Skye Tate, a smalltown girl living a quiet, simple life. I live at home with my Mum, Bev, and am content to tick along without too much fuss. I have no big dreams or ambitions and can't see myself doing anything different to what I'm doing right now.

Mum will have dinner in the fridge for me, glad wrap over the top, ready to be reheated in the microwave. It's Friday night and she's at the members draw and raffles at the RSL Club. I called earlier to let her know I wouldn't be coming, and to pass on a message to my best friend Candy, who has been badgering me all week to go out with her to the pub, that I am staying home tonight. I am working early in the morning, and besides, I'm halfway through the latest Nicholas Sparks novel, *The Notebook*, and can't wait to read the next chapter.

I don't hear Quinton and startle when I see him standing in the doorway.

'Hey,' he says.

'Hey, Quinton! You frightened me!'

He smiles with his eyes. Quinton doesn't waste words, the opposite to me. A chatterbox, who fills in all the blank spaces.

'I'm just about to head home. All the girls are settled in for the night.'

He nods. When he still doesn't speak, I start to walk towards the door to head home.

'How do you think things are going?' he asks, out of the blue. 'You know, you've been here so long, you've got a good handle on things.' He stumbles over his words. 'This is all new to us. We probably aren't doing as good a job as what Austin's parents did...'

I jump in reassuringly. 'You're doing brilliantly, honestly. You and Beth are doing a great job.'

I watch his face closely to see if there's any reaction to Beth's name. He doesn't give anything away and I keep babbling. 'I'd have to say they're doing a lot better since you started shifting more of them out of the stalls and giving them room to move.'

'Yeah, they seem happier.'

'They do. That's a brilliant idea. You have so many orders to fill, the happier the pigs are the better they'll breed, it's just better all round.'

'I can't take all the credit. Beth reckons we need to invest while things are going well and keep up the momentum Austin's parents have started.'

Quinton's voice shakes, the tiniest amount.

'Exactly,' I say brightly, instinctively wanting to make him feel better. A long silence follows and again I fill it. 'There's lots of reasons for putting them in stalls, but I have to say, I never really liked seeing the girls locked up like that. I understand the productivity side of it, but it seems so cruel, you know?'

'Yeah.' Quinton nods.

'If you put them outside, I guess what you need to be mindful of is making sure you don't ruin the paddocks. Pigs can be pretty hard on the environment, especially when you have so many. So many hills too, and we get a fair bit of run-off when it rains...' my voice tapers off, worried I am overstepping in my effort to fill his long silences.

I have a secret passion for the environment and when I left high school I completed a short course at the Permaculture College at Nimbin, after seeing it advertised in the paper. I read any soil book I can find and am picking up the threads of concern in some circles that modern farming practices are ruining them. It worries me to see so many farmers in this area using high doses of chemicals and fertilisers to chase higher yields for pasture and grain crops, even Austin's parents.

'Run-off is a whole new thing for me. Out west it's mostly flat. Run-off is never an issue.'

Conversation halts.

'You want a beer?' Quinton asks, opening the fridge.

'Oh, no, I'm okay, thanks.'

He moves closer, smelling fresh and clean. I'm not the only one just out of the shower.

'You sure? I'm having one.'

'Okay, I'll stay for one beer.'

'What's on for tonight?' he asks casually, passing me an ice-cold XXXX can.

'Not much. Mum goes down to the club every Friday night for the members draw and raffles. I usually go with her, but I didn't quite get finished in time, so I'll probably just go home and have the dinner she's most likely got sitting in the fridge for me.'

'That's something my Mum would do too,' he chuckles, a deep chuckle I hear every now and then around the sheds, mostly when he's with Austin.

'I'm spoilt, Mum's a bit of a fusser. She doesn't like it if I don't eat properly, she's always trying to fatten me up.'

Quinton looks me up and down. 'It's not working,' he says, then blushes. 'Sorry, I didn't mean to...'

'That's okay, I don't mind,' I say softly, unable to stop myself from flirting.

'You know, you can knock off early if you've got something to go to, don't you? Especially on a Friday night. You're young, I'm sure there's a nightlife in town you're part of.'

'I know, but with everyone else having to go, I didn't want to leave you in the lurch. As to partying on a Friday night, I love my nights out but I'm just as happy at home curled up on the couch with a good book.'

I blush, worried I sound boring.

'Is there much to do around here on a weekend?' he asks. 'Beth and I have been planning to get into town and meet a few people but haven't yet, with her work in the city...' His voice tremors again.

'It's okay, I like it. There's a bit going on. Depends what you're into. Footy season is a lot of fun. Do you play?'

'Yes and no, I'm not that good. I've played a few games, mostly when I was younger. I was more interested in rodeoing.'

'Younger? You're such an old man, what would you be, twenty-five?' I laugh. He doesn't reply. Looks like I'll have to keep guessing his age.

'Cheers.' I offer my widest, most cheerful smile.

He lifts his can slightly and winks. Not just any wink, an Aussie cowboy wink which rates a ten out of ten in the heart melting department.

I admire his brilliant blue eyes and strong jawline, and get the faint whiff of his deodorant. Lynx Africa. I know it well – all the young men around town wear it.

'Are you okay, Quinton?'

He doesn't answer.

'She doesn't deserve you, you know.'

The words are out before I can stop them, words I've been wanting to say all day. Beth doesn't care about him the way a woman needs to care about her man. The way I would care for him. I would dote on him, dedicate every waking moment to his needs.

His eyes glisten as he looks into his beer can.

I hold my breath, not sure what to do next or where this conversation is going.

He looks up to see me staring. I part my lips and smile.

2

QUINTON

I can't look away from her dark brown eyes with long, black lashes which seem to fill her whole face. She has a small button nose and slightly olive skin which sets off a wide, bright smile that lights up the room. Everything about her is slender and lithe; she recently told me she's a runner and in training for a triathlon. She is wearing a low-cut T-shirt and shorts and her long, lean legs go on forever.

I drain my beer and break the moment to go to the fridge for another.

'Here,' I say, turning to offer her one. While my back was turned she had moved silently towards me and we're face to face, so close I can smell the shampoo in her hair.

She is shorter, but not by much.

'No, I don't want another one,' she says, quietly. 'I want you.'

I feel the cold air from the fridge on my back and awkwardly return the second can. I move past her to lean against the bench, out of reach.

She moves gracefully to boldly stand in front of me. She takes the beer out of my hand and places it deliberately on the bench, brushing her fingers against mine and sending thrills to my boot-clad feet.

Slowly, she reaches down to touch my fingers, one side and then the other, and intertwines hers through mine. I still haven't moved. She looks up to catch my eyes on her cleavage.

I flush. 'I'm sorry.'

She smiles. 'That's okay. I don't mind if you look.'

I start to pull my hands away, but she holds them tight and moves closer until our bodies are touching the full length of each other.

'Like I said,' she whispers, 'I don't mind if you look.'

I look again and know she can feel me harden against her leg. She still has my hands and body trapped against the bench.

She softly kisses me on the side of my neck, breathing in my scent before reaching up to cup my face. I am freshly shaven, and she moves her hands over my cheeks.

'So smooth,' she whispers into my mouth. 'I love sitting on a smooth face.'

I gasp inwardly, unsure if I've heard correctly. My cock has, though, and is desperate to get out of my jeans. She is breathing heavily and although I'm trying to hold back and resist this beautiful young woman offering herself to me, I give in and kiss her back, hungrily, moving my hands behind her head to run them through her long, beautiful hair. I grab a handful and pull her closer, my tongue probing and circling in her mouth as I get lost in the moment.

Her hands go to my top button, then the next and the next. I let go of her hair so she can pull my shirt off and place gentle kisses on my neck and down my chest. My hands can't stop. They're all over her body, up and down her back, on her arse cheeks, then reaching underneath the back of her skimpy singlet to undo her bra so I can watch her petite breasts fall free.

She stops me, and with her mouth back on mine, she whispers, *slow down, I want to make this last.*

I don't want to slow down. I want her, right now, hard and fast. I want to rip her shirt and shorts off, lay her on the table, and be inside her. But she has me pinned and I am unable to move. I struggle, surprised by her strength. She is in complete control.

She whispers in my ear. 'Have you got any idea how long I've wanted this?'

I groan, wriggling to get free, but she keeps her strong hold on my arms.

Without letting go, she returns to kissing my chest, then moves further down, down. I close my eyes as her kisses send shivers of desire through me, and with every kiss going lower, I feel myself getting harder. I am desperate for her to undo my belt and zip and let me out.

Eventually, when I'm about to blow, she lets go of my hands. I hold my breath, waiting expectantly for her to go where I am willing her to go, but instead she stands and puts those beautiful lips on mine, her tongue probing as she reaches for my hands again, gently this time, and guides them inside my jeans with hers.

'Mmmm,' she groans. 'Feel how hard you are.'

Her fingers flick over my wet tip while she moves one of my hands to cup my balls and the other to grip the full length, still confined inside my jeans and wanting to burst free.

She takes her wet finger and puts it in our mouths which are still joined, and I taste my saltiness for the first time.

'Tastes good, doesn't it?' she moans as she moves her finger around my mouth.

'I've never tasted it before,' I admit, panting for breath.

'You don't know what you've been missing,' she says, reaching down for more.

I take my hands out so I can pull her closer, grabbing her hair again, kissing her deeply, wanting to get inside her. She pulls her hand out and steps away, placing the wetness dribbling out of my tip onto my tongue, watching me lick and suck it from her finger.

She is still in charge.

Instinctively, I know she wants me to beg. I'm ready to beg.

Without breaking my gaze, finally she undoes my belt, top button and zip and with her feet, deftly pushes my jeans and boxers down to the floor. I kick my boots off and step out of them. Her eyes widen as she admires me, vulnerable and fully naked.

'You are the most gorgeous cowboy I have ever laid eyes on. The real deal, smoking hot,' she says as she rubs her hands all over my back, chest and arse cheeks.

I tell her with my eyes that I want, no I need, her to cup my balls with one hand and pump my shaft with the other. She knows exactly what I need and watches me closely as she grips my cock tightly and gently squeezes my balls.

'You also have the biggest cock I've ever held in my hands,' she says, watching it grow bigger at her touch.

I use the bench to hold me up as she kneels down, guiding me into her mouth. I want to come then and there.

'What are you doing to me?' I groan.

She sucks, licks and when she only has the head inside her mouth, she puts her hands on my arse cheeks and pulls me roughly towards her until she chokes.

'Fuck my mouth,' she demands the next time she pulls away. 'Fuck it hard until you hear me choke.'

I groan louder and louder, grabbing desperately at her, wanting to strip her naked and feel her skin on mine, but I can't reach.

She is still in total control. As commanded, I fuck it, harder and harder until she chokes and gags. She stands to kiss me, using her tongue on mine to make sure I can taste what she's tasting.

'I have to touch you,' I say. 'I have to have those beautiful, round tits in my mouth.'

'How badly do you want to touch me?' she asks, pulling away so we're not touching at all.

I watch her take off her T-shirt.

'So badly,' I beg, moving towards her, but she moves further away.

'I need more begging. I want you to want me so badly you would do anything to have me.'

'I would do anything,' I say, admiring the way her plain black bra holds her breasts in place above her long, toned torso. I can see her nipples go hard through the fabric and groan. 'Anything.'

'Make your cock harder,' she demands, and watches me reach down to grab my long shaft and jerk it two or three times. Smiling, she reaches behind to unclasp her bra and her beautiful breasts spill out. I shift my hands so I can catch them, they're firm and soft at the same time. I brush my fingers over her nipples, watching in satisfaction as she flushes and tips her head back.

'My turn,' I growl with gravel in my voice. Effortlessly I lift her to sit on the edge of the table, before greedily putting one breast into my mouth and cupping the other, running my tongue over and around her nipple. When I am satisfied one is peaked enough, I move to the other, then push them together so I can try and get them both into my mouth at the same time.

In a feeble attempt to regain control, she spreads her legs and moves me off her breasts to watch her reach up through the bottom of her shorts.

I smirk, pushing her onto her back and roughly spread her legs so I can move her G-string aside to plunge and curl my fingers inside her. She melts at my touch. I have her exactly where I want her.

'You're dripping wet,' I say, leaning over to continue sucking her nipples while slowly pushing two fingers in and out, in and out. I go deep, watching her face the deeper I go. She is breathing hard and her eyes glaze over.

I lift her down onto a chair so I can kneel and get better access to her swollen wetness. With her shorts pushed aside I continue to push my fingers in and out, harder and faster, not letting her look away. She is making mewling noises and starts to beg, pulling at me.

When she pulls my wet fingers out of her so she can taste them, that is it. I must have my tongue inside her. I stand her up so and she undoes her shorts and steps out of them.

'You are so beautiful,' I say as she stands before me in a plain black G string. I turn her around and go down on my knees, pulling her G string aside before plunging my tongue into her from behind.

Skye is rubbing her hands over her breasts, her eyes closed, and I know she is close to coming. I pull down her G-string and she steps out of it before I roughly turn her around to lift her onto the table and spread her wide.

I admire her before I lean down and as soon as my tongue licks the full length of her lips, she arches her back and cries out. I go softly and gently on her clit and my hands join hers to touch her breasts. I lick, suck, nibble and thrust with my tongue while enjoying the feel of her breasts and peaked nipples.

'Is your cock hard?' she asks breathlessly. 'I need it in my mouth.'

I climb onto the table and fuck her mouth, twice as hard as before. She has hold of my arse, pulling my cheeks apart, touching my balls from behind, and finding a sweet spot I didn't know existed.

She pulls me in so she can put my full length in her mouth. I sit over her while she sucks hungrily and greedily, her fingers digging into my arse until I can feel pain.

'You want to come all over my face, don't you?' she pants between sucks.

I do, but I'm not done yet. I pull out of her mouth and slide down to kiss her. She grabs at me as I move my mouth onto one breast and then the other.

as I tease her nipples with my tongue.

I drag my tongue down her stomach, then lower until it is resting on her clit, motionless, waiting. I tease, putting my tongue for the briefest of moments on her clit, then off. She runs her fingers through my hair and tries to push me down further and force my tongue inside her, but I resist. When she comes, I want her to scream the shed down.

'I'm so close, oh, oh, I can't wait any longer, I'm going to come.'

She starts to whimper. 'I need your tongue, all of it. I want your tongue inside me, now, please. I need it, I want it, I want to come. *Now.*'

I smile, my tongue infuriatingly close. I didn't think it was possible to get any harder, but the thought of how desperately she wants this is like fuel to my flame.

She lifts her hips and when I know she is on the edge, I thrust my tongue deep inside. With loud screams she trembles and I feel her grab my tongue. Tasting her salty, sweet stickiness, I lay with my tongue resting inside her until I know she's got nothing left.

I stand and pull her gently into the sitting position, my face covered in her wetness. She kisses me and licks every bit of herself off my face.

It drives me wild as she revels in her taste and my cock is the hardest it's ever been.

'I don't have a condom,' I whisper. 'Can I come in your mouth?'

Skye kisses me, harder, her hands all over my cock, and whispers back. 'I love it up the arse.'

Her words send a jolt to my core, and it takes every inch of willpower for me not to let go there and then all over her hands.

She rolls over and onto her knees, parting her arse cheeks. This is new territory. I have fantasised about it, and Beth and I have been saying it more and more in the throes of the moment, but we have never gone that far.

Beth.

She appears before me and the effect is like a cold shower. My hard-on dissipates, and my brain spins out of control as I come to my senses and become aware of my surroundings.

The full beer sitting on the bench that Skye took out of my hands. The salty taste on my lips. The timber smoko table, which held strong in the throes of our passion. What am I doing?

I look at Skye's beautiful, welcoming body and gently pull her off the table.

She looks down, noticing my erection is gone.

Fully naked and exposed, I turn away and reach for my clothes, my face red from embarrassment. What would Beth say if she knew what I was doing, on our property, in our smoko room?

We haven't had a normal conversation for a long time, let alone shared a bed or a kind word. This morning she drove away without a backward glance, leaving me wondering if she'll ever return. Still, this gives me no right to be doing what I am doing.

I feel like a right royal jerk. I still have my back to Skye as I put on my shirt, slowly doing up my buttons while trying to regain my composure.

I can hear her gathering her clothes and getting dressed. Finally, I muster the courage to face her. 'I'm really sorry, Skye. I shouldn't have...'

She interrupts my clumsy apology. 'It's okay, Quinton, it's okay. I don't need you to say anything more.'

We stand awkwardly, both feeling the pull of the intimacy we just shared.

'No, no, I do,' I say. 'It's just that...' I am going redder than the apples from Mum's orchard. 'I've never done that before,' I blurt, deciding I was in enough of an awkward situation and I may-as-well be honest.

Her eyes tear up and I want to lift her into my arms and carry her inside, but know it is wrong.

I start tidying up; putting the beer back in the fridge and my empty can into the recycling bin. There's nothing more I can say. I need to get out of here to be with my own thoughts and feelings and figure out where the fuck I am at, and what the fuck I am doing.

3

SKYE

I slip away quietly, extremely embarrassed, but not wanting to show it.

I want him to think it's no big deal, that I'm in complete control of my emotions.

Tears stream down my cheeks at the memory of his touch, of his tongue. I reach down to feel my wetness, not wanting to shower ever again, so I can keep the scent of him on my body.

I certainly don't want him to know how I have lived out almost every fantasy about him and that everything which happened back there was more than anything I could have ever imagined.

That he has escalated my obsession and adoration to a whole new level.

That if I can't be with him, I think I might die.

4

QUINTON

I look up at the ceiling from the bed in the spare room. I moved in here after finding photos of Beth with her ex-boyfriend at a dinner party, a party she'd neglected to tell me about. She assures me there's nothing between them and that she's only seen him the once, but what I can't figure out is why she has photos of them together.

I'm insanely jealous and it's driven a wedge between us that gets bigger every day.

I toss and turn, unable to sleep. I can still taste Skye, and every time I close my eyes, I see her.

The memory of her beautiful body, her neat, perky breasts, her taut, tight body and her arse cheeks spread wide are impossible to switch off.

I pump myself, rough and fast, as I imagine sliding into her tight arse, slowly at first, then faster, as she pushes back, letting me in deeper, screaming loudly, *fuck me from behind Quinton, fuck me hard, harder, harder.*

Now!

5

SKYE

I call Austin early.

'Hey Skye, what's up?'

'Not much, I can't get onto Quinton, he might have already gone to the sheds. Can you let him know Mum needs me to take her up to the hossie and that I won't be able to come in today?'

'No wuckas! I hope Bev is okay?'

'Yeah, she's fine I think. She had a few chest pains through the night, she reckons it's nothing serious but a check-up won't hurt, even if it's nothing,' I say, the lies rolling off my tongue like maple syrup.

'That's no good. Hopefully it's nothing.'

'Thanks, Austin. Could you apologise to Quinton for me, you know, for letting him down?'

'I'm sure he won't see it like that,' Austin says. 'We'll be right. We'll survive without you.'

'Yeah, yeah. Not sure if you will, but you could try.'

I tiptoe back to my bedroom, not wanting to wake Mum, and hide under the covers. I didn't sleep a wink all night, visions of Quinton keeping me awake. I have blown it completely. What will he think of me? Did I really ask him to do that? It's not something you do on a first date. But to me, it didn't feel like a first date. It felt perfectly natural to ask him to do that.

As last night spirals around my head like a spinning top, I finally drop off into a deep, dreamless sleep.

...

MUM's persistent tapping on my door drags me from the depths.

'Are you right, Skye?'

'Mmmmm,' I mumble, not awake enough to get any words out.

Undeterred, Mum continues to talk through the door at her usual frenetic pace.

'I thought you were working today. I only just realised you haven't gone, I've been sidetracked in the garden. Are you sick?'

'I'm fine, Mum, but I've called Austin and he's covering my shift. Just got a bit of a cold or something and couldn't rally.'

'Okay, love, want me to come in and check your temperature?'

'No Mum, I'm just napping. I'm okay.'

'Are you sure? I can whip up a chicken soup – do you feel like chicken soup?'

As much as I love Mum's chicken soup, no I do not feel like chicken soup.

'No, I'm not hungry. Maybe later, I'll let you know.'

'Okay then love, I'll just be out in the garden if you need anything.'

It is just Mum and I; it has always been that way. Dad took off when I was so young that I can't even remember him. He's made no contact, and I've always had a vague understanding our lives are better off without him.

Mum doesn't have a selfish bone in her body and works three jobs to keep a roof over our heads, Her life lessons are simple. Work hard, don't lie, brush your teeth twice a day and be kind.

Although I was never at the top of the class, I worked hard at school. I have perfect teeth, thanks to the twice daily brushing and good genes. I never lie, apart from today.

I'm not overly ambitious and don't have big dreams or goals of studying, moving away or travelling the world. I love my hometown; my community, my friends, Mum's friends, and our close-knit network that is a constant stream in and out our front door.

Sport takes up a big part of my life. Running, bike riding and swimming. I like crime, romance and historical fiction novels. My favourite television show is *Friends* and my best girlfriend is Candy. I love to go out on a Friday and Saturday night to the pub and dance with the local boys, and every now and then, go home with one of them to satisfy my sexual urges with no strings attached.

Mum and I are close. We enjoy going down to the club for the members draw and raffles, and when I'm on a day off, I love nothing more than early morning gardening sessions followed by bingo with her and her crazy friends who know how to laugh, joke and have a rollicking good time.

I can't get back to sleep and contemplate my life. I had a couple of wild years starting in my last year of high school, always looking for the next adventure, the next thing to try that I probably shouldn't be trying. During this time I hooked up with my first serious boyfriend, Jackson, who was several years older than me.

Jackson.

Popular around town, a great conversationalist and exuberant storyteller. He was never interested in conversation with me. Instead, he instructed me on how to touch and love every inch of myself with his insatiable appetite for sex during our tumultuous, thrilling, exciting, two-year relationship.

I'd hear him coming from a mile away in his rumbling V8 Holden Commodore and the minute I opened the door I knew exactly what he wanted as he undressed me with his eyes. He couldn't wait to get me into the car and around to his place, which he shared with a bunch of mates, and whisk me into his bedroom.

He would tell me I was the most intriguing and stunning girl he had ever met, that he adored my heady mix of innocence, strong-will, independence and eagerness to please. He lived out his every sexual fantasy with me and I fell madly, deeply in love.

He broke, *shattered*, my heart when he accepted a job in the mines in Western Australia, saying we should free ourselves of the commitment to each other because I was so young.

I tried to hide my heartbreak and did my best to move on from my first true love. Each time he returned on leave, I'd fall back into his arms, happy to go along with his expectation that my world centred around him, and that I would always be waiting to pick up from where we left off. Which I was. Until Quinton strode into my life with his broad shoulders, deep voice, intoxicating cowboy hat and dazzling eyes.

Quinton is the opposite to Jackson. Softer, quieter, gentler. He doesn't say much but is genuinely curious and interested in hearing about people's lives. In one of our very first conversations he asked about my goals and dreams and what I liked to do in my spare time. My hobbies, interests, favourite movies, books and music.

He listens, intently. As though everything I say is important. I've never met a man like him.

The more time I spend around Quinton, the more my relationship with Jackson appears shallow. It is, and always has been, about the sex. I love the sex, but there has never been a meeting of our minds.

I have steadily built Quinton into the perfect man. It's not just his brooding cowboy vibe. He's made me realise I want to be with someone I can hold a conversation with, who is interested in my mind, interested in me.

I groan loudly, sick of being in my head, and force myself out of bed. I get dressed and make two cups of tea and carry them out into the garden. It is a gloriously warm spring day. The kind of day I usually feel grateful for.

Mum is kneeling in the vegetable garden.

'There you are. You look a bit pale, love.'

'I really am fine, Mum. I just didn't sleep very well.'

'I hope I didn't disturb you when I got home, I had a few drinks with the girls, and stayed out later than I intended,' Bev explains, even though she knows she doesn't need to explain when we are two adult women living adult lives.

'I didn't hear you; I must have been asleep then but woke later.' Here I am, lying again. Whenever either of us come home after the other, regardless of the hour, we always look in and more often than not, end up having a long chat about our respective days.

I was wide awake when Mum came home but pretended to be asleep because my mind and body were a bundle of feelings, nerves and emotions. I didn't trust myself not to blurt it all out and I knew what she would say.

Like everyone in the district, Mum knows all about Quinton and Beth buying the pig farm. She would not be happy to know I am a relationship wrecker. She is big on honesty, loyalty and integrity. I wouldn't be able to explain that every time I look at Quinton, all my integrity goes out the window.

Sometimes I hate Beth with a passion because she is in my way. I believe Quinton and I belong together. I am obsessed and have to fight the urge to tell him how I feel every time we are in the same room.

I am sounding so desperate. I don't want him to think I am desperate. I'm not desperate in the true sense of the word. As well as Jackson on his home visits, I have no shortage of male suitors, but none of them are Quinton. They all seem like young boys, immature and weak. None of them match up to this tall, strong cowboy from the far-flung outback who has landed himself right in front of me. He is my destiny, I just know it.

'I hope you haven't let them down at work today, that Quinton and Beth couple,' Mum says as she sits with legs folded on the ground, sipping her tea. 'They're such a lovely couple, having a real go. It's so nice to see young people working hard and having new faces bring new energy and ideas to our town.'

I resist the urge to roll my eyes.

'No Mum, Austin's doing my shift for me. I've covered for him plenty of times.'

'That's good, as long as you've got some understanding that those pigs need constant care and attention.'

'Yes, I know Mum.'

Bev sits her tea cup on the timber railway sleeper that edges the garden bed and goes back to planting a row of corn.

'How are they going out there? Settling in okay? I haven't seen them go out in town much, I occasionally see them at the supermarket or chemist but thought they might come in for a meal at the club or something,' Bev says.

The sun warms me from the inside out and I push away my irritation, needing to keep up the guise everything was normal when nothing felt normal anymore.

'I reckon they're too busy for a social life. Quinton has got a lot of great ideas. He wants to change things out there and I believe he will make it better.'

'Really? I thought they had a pretty good system going, Susan and Fred have always had a very successful business.'

'Yeah, well, they did but he wants to do it differently.'

I'd picked up on the many conversations between Austin and Quinton in the smoko room where Quinton outlined his plans and ideas and watched him drive off in the ute packed with fencing gear to fix fences and make smaller pig paddocks, as well as pull down fences to make bigger pasture paddocks.

'He's planning to free range the pigs and change the way they grow their pastures, it's fascinating what he's wanting to do. All the big city restaurants and supermarkets...' I taper off, Mum isn't even listening.

'There, corn's done,' Bev says, patting her gloved hands together before picking up her tea for another sip. 'You make a good cuppa, love.'

'Thanks Mum.'

'Next to plant are carrots and radishes. We're going to have a good veggie crop come summer,' Mum continues, planting a new row of teensy tiny carrot seeds.

'After I get this done, I'm off to a bread baking class but before that I have to do a few hours at the club.'

'You're on lunch shifts this week?'

'Yes, frees me up at night.'

'Frees you up for a hot date,' I tease.

'Not too many hot dates in this town.'

'True. Same old, same old.'

'You think it's same old, same old for your age. You wait until you get to my age. Slim pickings, for sure.' Mum cackles her famous cackle and I laugh with her.

'There is Bill, though. He's pretty sweet on you.'

'Bill and I are good friends. I am not ready to settle down just yet.'

'You are settled down, Mum. Bill can give you a bit of company when I'm not here. And a bit of something else!'

'Skye! Stop it! I'm not going to talk about that with you,' Bev scolds, a smile in her voice.

'You're only human, and it's only natural,' I say emphatically.

Mum shakes her head.

'You young ones, you're so open.'

'It's better than being a closed shop like you've been for the past twenty years,' I say cheekily, but know I've pushed the envelope. 'Anyway, I'm going to have a shower and some food, and then I think I'll go for a run.'

...

As a perfect spring day turns into a cool evening, perfect for curling up on the couch with a good book, I ignore the phone ringing in the kitchen. Mum is over at Bill's for dinner, enjoying the freshly-baked bread she made in her cooking class. I politely declined the invitation to join them. I'd managed to keep busy for most of the day but I wasn't up for anyone's company.

I am tempted to leave it but then thought it might be Mum with something urgently important, which was usually not that important, but important to her.

'Hello, Skye speaking,' I say breathlessly after a last-minute dash.

'Skye speaking, it's Quinton speaking.'

I drop my book on the ground.

'Quinton.'

Long pause.

'I'm sorry, sorry I didn't come to work today,' I splutter.

'That's okay,' he says awkwardly. 'It was probably good that you didn't, you know, give us a bit of time to...' The rest of his sentence disappears into thin air.

'How'd things go?' I ask. 'Did I miss anything?'

'Not really, just the usual. Got a bit of fencing done at the end of the day.'

An hour later we're still talking about the pigs and Quinton's plans for the farm. It's the longest conversation we've ever had and I am hanging off every word. I picture him, all alone in the large split-level family home which Austin grew up in, with nobody to talk to. He must get so lonely.

'... and I have been reading all these soil books from America and think I will grow a few different plant species in the paddocks, keep the soil covered and focus on increasing the soil biology,' Quinton explains. 'Sorry Skye, you must be so bored.'

'No, really, go on. I find it fascinating.'

'I was never much good at school, all I wanted to do was be outside and I didn't really try,' he says. 'You couldn't get me to pick up a book when I was at school. But all this stuff about soil, I can't put the books down. I could read all day.'

There's a long pause, waiting for someone to fill.

'I like reading too,' I say. 'I'm reading a good book at the moment.'

'What's it about?'

I look down at the book I dropped on the floor earlier.

'It's called *The Notebook*. It's an, um, romance.'

I am blushing and the longer the silence from the other end of the line, the redder I go. Quinton coughs awkwardly.

'Speaking of romance,' he says, 'that's the reason for my call.'

My stomach flips over itself.

'It's just that, you know... Beth.'

'Yes?' I can't keep the testiness from my voice.

'It's just that, well, we've been having a few problems,' Quinton confesses. 'I shouldn't be talking to you about it, but I also shouldn't be dragging you into it. We've been together for a long time, and we have a lot of things tying us together...'

I cut him off.

'You're too nice for her,' I blurt out. 'But you don't need to worry about me. You might not know how you feel but I know exactly how I feel.'

The silence goes on for so long that I wonder if he's hung up on me.

Eventually he asks, 'how *do* you feel?'

I lower my voice. 'I feel like one day I'd really like it if you fucked me up the arse.'

I hang up slowly, leaving Quinton on the other end of the line to wonder if he has heard me correctly.

6

QUINTON

Did she really say that?

I look down at my giant erection and it's all I can do to not blow right there and then.

This is not where I was expecting this conversation to end up.

I've never been much good with words, or long conversations. Especially with the opposite sex.

My plan was to apologise for my behavior and tell Skye clearly and succinctly that although Beth and I aren't in a good place, we haven't officially called it quits. I'd planned to explain I'd never been unfaithful, it wasn't my style, and I should never have let things go as far as they did.

I was planning to say it would never, could never, happen again.

All my plans have flown out the window.

All I want to do is drive into town to Skye's house and do exactly what she says she wants me to do.

Instead, I go to the bathroom to relieve the pressure, visions of Skye and Beth blurring into one as I shoot all over the shower screen.

7

SKYE

I keep my distance, Quinton too, and we never speak of the tearoom or phone conversation again. It's strictly business between us. I'm hurting but I refuse to let on.

He makes sure we are never alone and leaves the sheds early to go fencing or mow the lawns in the homestead garden. I wonder if he knows I used to spend every afternoon and weekends in the garden with Austin's Mum, Susan.

Since she left it has fallen into disrepair, and it breaks my heart every time I drive in for my shift to see the state it's in.

I have been taking tea and lunch breaks at different times to the others but today Mum has sent me to work with a basket of fresh vegetables. I sneak it in when I think nobody is around but come across Austin and Quinton quietly studying the For Sale pages in *The Land* newspaper.

'Oh, hi,' I say shyly.

'Skye!' Austin greets me with his usual boyish enthusiasm. 'What have you got there? It looks like you and Bev have been busy in the garden again.'

I laugh, focusing on Austin and trying not to look at Quinton.

'Mostly Bev, but yes, me too. We can't keep up with harvesting it all and Bev wants you boys to eat more vegetables! There's enough there to last you two a week, then some for Monty and Adeline.'

Austin starts looking through the basket. 'Hey Quinton, did you happen to notice the veggie patch near the tool shed? If we couldn't find Mum and Skye around the sheds, that was always the next spot we'd check. There's only one woman in the district who can match Mum's green thumb in the veggie garden and that's Bev, closely followed by Skye.'

'You like gardening?' Quinton asks.

'Yes, I love it,' I say shyly. 'Mum and I have a smallish garden, not even close to the size of the one out here, but we grow veggies to sell at the local market. We don't use any chemicals; Susan never did either. We make our compost and use different plants to control any pests. And we use the pig manure from here to keep the soil in good condition.'

Quinton raises his eyebrows.

'So, all that stuff I was telling you about the paddocks, you do it already in your garden?'

'Yep, sure do.'

Quinton blushes.

'You could too, it wouldn't be hard to reinvigorate the garden out here,' I offer. 'Mum grows seedlings as well and I could bring some out. And as you know, you have plenty of pig poo.'

'That would be great,' Quinton says, his eyes lighting up. 'I haven't gotten to the veggie patch yet.' He turns to Austin. 'I feel bad, mate, about your Mum's garden. Beth and I have been trying to get it back in order, she was making a fair headway out in the garden, but her work has her tied down at the moment.'

I see Quinton flush and take it as my cue to leave but Quinton calls me back.

'Skye, the pig poo thing. You reckon I could put that on the paddocks?' He pulls out the chair next to him in invitation. I slowly lower myself into the chair, careful not to touch legs.

'Yes, you could. Mum reckons it's the best pig poo on earth. The biggest challenge would be how to spread it and the time it would take. You can't exactly spread it with a shovel on a big paddock like you do on a garden patch.'

'I know a bloke with a spreader,' Austin offers. 'He might be worth talking to.'

The way Quinton's eyes light up rival the sun. I watch him scribble notes at a frenetic pace.

'I'd better get back to work,' I say, knowing Quinton will be here for some time.

'Thanks, great. Yes, I'd love some seedlings if you have some and thank your Mum for the veggies. Beth and I won't waste them.'

Quinton doesn't look up from his notebook as he talks, his mind racing at a million miles an hour. Austin laughs as he follows me out to the sheds, slapping Quinton on the back as we go.

'We'll leave you with it, mate, I can see you've got some new ideas to add to that growing 'ideas pile' of yours, Beth won't be able to keep up.'

'Mmm,' Quinton mumbles as we leave.

'There's no stopping him,' Austin says as we walk to shed number four. 'The energy and enthusiasm of that man knows no limits.'

'Must make you feel good, you know, to have this place in good hands.'

'Absolutely. We got lucky when this incredible young couple set their sights on being pig farmers. I can't wait to see where Quinton and Beth take it.'

I don't answer, I can't. I'm trying to hide my heartbreak at being the third wheel. What am I thinking to imagine I have any right to be part of Quinton's life in any other way apart from being his employee?

I might have fallen madly and deeply in love, but he has his life already mapped out. Even if he and Beth are having problems, he isn't going to walk away from his plans for little old me. And I'm certainly not going to wait around for him.

With my head held high and shoulders back, I finish my shift with renewed vigour and enthusiasm. Time to move on – what happened between us happened but that's all it will ever be. I am an idiot to think it could be anything else.

8

SKYE

Just like the old days, I can hear his rumbling V8 Holden Commodore, the latest model, coming from several blocks away.

I am waiting at the door, ready to open on his first knock. Again, just like the old days.

I take a sharp intake of breath. Damn. I'd forgotten how good-looking Jackson was. He looks even fitter from his physically demanding job in the mines. And tall, a full head taller than me. I have always loved the way he towers over me.

'Hey, Skye,' he winks, and my knees buckle.

'Hey, Jackson.'

Without further ado, he moves in for a hug and kisses me behind the ear in the place that makes my legs feel like jelly.

'You're hotter than I remember,' he says as he breathes into my ear and reaches around to grab my arse, lifting me off the ground with ease and squeezing me close. 'That smile of yours is stunning.'

'Still the charmer,' I laugh, returning the hug.

'Hey, Mum, Jackson's here,' I call out, ushering him inside.

'G'day Bev, you're looking younger than the day I first met you,' he grins as he leans down to give Mum a hug.

'Hello Jackson, still the charmer,' Bev says wryly. 'You haven't lost any of that charm working out in the middle of nowhere.'

'There's nobody to charm out there so I've been saving it all for you.'

'You're smooth, just like your father,' Bev teases. Jackson's Dad runs the rural merchandise shop in town and he's always had an eye for the ladies.

'Skye, love, pop on the kettle, I'm sure Jackson has a lot of stories to catch us up on.'

I watch Mum regale Jackson with the latest gossip and stories he'd missed since he'd been away and entertain the thought of him sitting at this exact table enjoying cups of tea with Mum for years to come. Jackson shares an equal number of stories, and between the two of them I don't have a hope of getting a word in.

Eventually they both take a breath.

'What do you reckon, Skye? We might need to get going,' Jackson reaches under the table to put his hand on my leg, sending shivers through me. 'I've got a table booked at this new restaurant that's opened.'

'I hear the food's pretty fancy,' Bev says. 'They've got some chefs from Sydney or somewhere and it's the fanciest food Scone has ever seen.'

'It's good to have something apart from the local Chinese and a pub steak,' I say, gathering my things so we can get away from my chatty mother.

'I want to take my girl somewhere special,' Jackson says, winking at me. I feel slightly annoyed at his confidence. He thinks he can just waltz in and out as he pleases, assuming I am pining and waiting. Then again, maybe I shouldn't overthink it. There is a lot to like about him. His dark brown, almost black, hair, dark brown eyes, five-day stubble and toned and muscly arms that can lift me effortlessly. Not to mention his one dimple and square jawline.

At dinner Jackson can't keep his eyes off me as he talks non-stop about how good the money is in the mines.

'I never take much notice of town gossip but is it true you've bought a block of land and a house?' I ask as the neatly dressed waiter puts a white cloth napkin on my lap.

'True, all true. I've bought the grand old homestead home from Doctor Booth.'

'Nice. That's my favourite part of town and I love that house,' I say as I study the menu, which lists dishes I haven't heard of.

'It's real nice. The doctor's wife has done a lot of work in the past ten years and there's not much left to be done. I'd like to put in a pool and tennis court and build a new shed out the back to house all the toys I plan to buy and set up a man cave.'

Jackson is energetic about his future plans and I nod and smile at the appropriate times as I enjoy my sashimi entrée and main meal of fresh salmon with crispy skin and freshly steamed green vegetables that taste almost as good as what I eat at home, but not quite. I must see if they are interested in buying fresh from Bev, who has just built two new garden beds and planted them to beans, lettuces, herbs and tomatoes.

'You've done so well for yourself, Jackson. It must be isolated and lonely, though. So far from anywhere.'

'Yeah, it's pretty isolated. Not much to do apart from work. There's a fair bit of opportunity, you've just got to stick at it.'

'Everyone talks about how good the money is,' I say. 'Are there any jobs out there for women?'

'Not many, plus, it's pretty rough, a whole bunch of blokes from a whole bunch of backgrounds. A girl like you turns up and it could get dangerous. Or it could get fun,' he grins suggestively.

I laugh, relaxed in his familiar company. Maybe it's better to just put all my attention into Jackson, the arrangement could work quite well. Casual, easy, fun.

'If you were out there, you could keep me entertained in my downtime,' Jackson winks as he reaches his hand underneath the table to touch my bare leg. 'You look real pretty, Skye.'

'Thanks Jackson, you scrub up all right yourself,' admiring the way his tight-fitting, black T-shirt shows off his rugged good looks, muscly biceps and washboard stomach. Effortlessly casual. All that is missing is cowboy boots and an oversized shiny belt buckle. *Stop*, I tell myself. *Move on, forget about Quinton and be grateful for what Jackson offers.*

I move my legs slightly apart, and Jackson reaches further up my floral, flowy dress that falls halfway to my knees and dips down at the front to show off my cleavage. I move his hands between my thighs.

He looks up, his eyes wide. I'm not wearing any underwear, and I am perfectly smooth since Candy discovered a growing trend in the city at a hairdressing expo of the full bikini wax, making me be her practice client before she unleashed the *Brazilian* trend in tiny Scone.

'You want to skip dessert?' I ask.

I wait outside while Jackson pays, breathing in fresh night air laced with promise.

'How about we go dancing first?' I ask as he grabs my hand and pulls me towards the car. 'All the girls are out tonight, I said we might drop by.'

Jackson leans in and kisses me at that spot behind my ear. 'Is your best friend Candy going to be there?'

'Yes, she is,' I say, knowing why he is asking.

One night, years ago when he and I first met, we got blind drunk at one of his house parties and found ourselves in a threesome. Jackson has hinted more than once for a repeat but the experience stirred up so many mixed feelings that I've never wanted to go there again.

As soon as we're in the car Jackson has two fingers inside me, kissing me passionately as he roughly plunges in and out. When I close my eyes, I see Quinton with his tongue inside me and come within seconds.

Jackson puts his sticky fingers in our mouths.

'Didn't take you long,' he says into my open mouth, reaching down for more. I move his hands off me, still thinking of Quinton even though I know it's wrong.

'You're going to have to wait,' I say with control, 'I want you to want me so bad you can't breathe.'

'I can't breathe,' he says.

I flash him a teasing grin. 'You can wait. Take me dancing, Jackson.'

He groans as he starts up the car. 'Girl, you drive me wild.'

I throw my head back and laugh, pushing all thoughts of Quinton aside and forcing myself to live in this moment, far away from the place where my heart got shattered into little pieces.

...

'Skye!'

The loud, booming voice of my best friend in the whole world travels across the room above the loud music from the DJ who is cranking out classic eighties and nineties tracks from Roxette to ACDC to INXS to Nirvana.

Within seconds Candy has bowled me over in a big, crazy hug, managing to hug and keep a drink in each hand upright. It looks like she's been here for quite some time. She passes a drink to me and one to Jackson.

'Well, well, well, if it's not our Jackson back in town,' Candy says as she jumps up to wrap her arms around his neck and give him a sloppy kiss on the lips. An unexpected bolt of jealousy sends shivers through me.

Candy is half a head shorter than me, and has curves I can only dream of. We are the yin and yang – I'm slender, dark-haired and tall, she's curvy, blonde and short. I'm serious, quiet and usually think before I speak. She's loud, boisterous and always speaks before the thought has fully formed.

Jackson laughs as he gives my hand a reassuring squeeze, noticing how my body stiffens when Candy kisses him. 'Nice to see you too, Candy.'

She looks down at our hands.

'Sorry, Skye, I didn't realise you and Jackson were back to being an item. I'm not trying to cut in on your man,' she says with bubbles in her voice, downplaying her obvious excitement at seeing Jackson. 'Big reunion, is it?'

'Something like that,' Jackson says.

I close the door on my unwanted jealousy guest as Candy drags us to a table in the corner away from the loud speakers.

'We've just been out for dinner to that new place,' I say, unable to hide the sharp edges on my words despite knowing that she wasn't to know Jackson and I are hooking up again. The last conversation we'd had was about me refusing to wait around anymore. I had clearly stated that next time he pulled into my driveway I would tell him to back right out. I know she's always had a thing for him, even when he and I were officially dating.

'I haven't been there yet. I don't have some swanky boyfriend swanning into town to take me out to fancy restaurants.'

'We'll take you with us next time,' Jackson says.

'You bloody better, you're loaded.'

'Not currently loaded,' he says. 'Not after buying the old doctor's house. Cost me a fair penny.'

Candy knew all about Jackson buying Doctor Booth's house. As a hairdresser, there wasn't much she didn't know about the comings and goings in town.

'I'd have to say Jackson, it's not the kind of house I imagined you to buy,' Candy says. 'It's a family home, not a bachelor's pad. Thinking of settling down, are you?'

She looks again to see if we're still holding hands. We're not.

Jackson laughs. 'Nah. Just thought it was a good investment. I used to walk past that house when I was a kid and say to myself that one day I'd love me a house just like that. What do you know, it comes on the market, I'm all cashed up and I thought, well, I can make one of my dreams come true.'

'Good on you, mate,' Candy says. 'You've done well, but we bloody miss you around here, don't we, Skye?' She gets up and pulls us into a hug. 'Okay, enough talking. Who's ready for some dancing?'

I scull my drink, wanting to shake myself out of my head.

'I'm in!'

Jackson watches us twirl each other around, close dance with our arms wrapped around each other while we continually talk over the loud music. I look over to see him watching us with desire written all over his face. It takes me back to *that* night, not long after my eighteenth birthday. A night I pretended I was too drunk to remember; a night Candy, Jackson and I have never spoken of again...

...

Three years earlier

CANDY and I have been drinking for several hours by the time Jackson arrives to pick us up for his party.

He orders us to sit in the back, and we giggle and roll our eyes at him bossing us around.

'Looks like you girls have well and truly started your own party,' he says, looking at us in the rear vision mirror.

'Maybe baby,' I say as Candy wraps her arms around my neck and snuggles close. We've been best friends since primary school and at this point in our lives, fresh out of high school, we remain inseparable. Her part-time job in the hairdressing salon has turned into an apprenticeship and my part-time job at the pig farm has become full-time, leaving us our weekends to relax, unwind and party. I've been dating Jackson for a year or so and he knows the deal, Candy never gets left behind.

Unbeknown to us, seeing the two of us so close in his backseat has given Jackson a hard-on and he presses his foot to the accelerator, keen to get us to the party. We walk into a thick cigarette haze in a house full of twenty-five-year-olds swaying to loud music. There's a keg in the back yard, a pig on a spit and a spread of salads and cheese platters on a large trellis table on the concrete patio. Candy and I are the youngest and are familiar with these standard weekend get togethers after Saturday's football and netball games, where everyone spills out of the pub to this party house. These parties have been going for seven years, since Jackson turned eighteen, and have improved in more recent times with the inclusion of girlfriends and new wives.

Candy and I feel at home, on the cusp of our adult lives and landing right in the middle of where we know we'll be by the time we're twenty-five, married with children on the way.

As the night wears on into the morning, couples peel off and head home, leaving Jackson, Candy and I in the open plan lounge on the biggest couch in town which stretches along one wall and down another. A record player sits in the corner and Jackson picks one from the large cabinet underneath. I know it will be Fleetwood Mac, *Rumours*, it is his favourite.

'How many times have you played this record?' Candy teases, twirling and dancing to the sexy, husky voice of Stevie Nicks and her song about a witch, *Rhiannon*.

Jackson hands me a rum and coke.

'I feel like I'm in a movie,' I say to nobody in particular.

'You are in a movie,' Jackson says, wrapping his arms around me and putting his hands up the bottom of my skirt, touching my ass then moving his fingers around the front to flick my clit. 'Just like the movie we watched last week.' He winks at me and kisses me on the neck knowingly. He's talking about the new porn movie he asked me to watch with him, which led us to one of the hottest and horniest sex sessions I've experienced.

I take another long sip of my drink and hand it back to Jackson.

'You've gotten more gorgeous since the last time I saw you,' he says.

'That was only yesterday,' Candy giggles as she joins us. Jackson moves aside and takes Candy's hands and guides them to the top button on my button-through singlet. She looks me deeply in the eyes as she starts unbuttoning. I stare back, my senses on fire and not disliking what she is doing.

'Like I said,' Jackson whispers with his hot breath in my ear. 'We're in a movie.'

The room swirls as she pushes the top of my bra down to release my breast and I am desperate for her to touch it. She moves her mouth onto my nipple and I groan in pleasure. Jackson, still standing behind me, runs his hands over my bare arse and slides his finger through to my clit, taking my wetness back to my arse and rubbing the tight hole he tells me his cock is going to fuck later. I'm tingling in a mix of apprehension and excitement, my brain trying to tell me this is not what nice girls do while my body begs for more.

Jackson moves me slowly to the long couch while Candy continues to touch, suck and lick my nipples which are free of my top and bra. Jackson pulls my skirt down and I'm completely naked as he pushes me onto my back and pulls my legs apart. He's still fully dressed, Candy too, and he commands Candy to kneel next to me and keep licking my nipples. While my body is on fire from what Candy is doing, I focus intently on Jackson as he removes his shirt and throws it into the corner before putting his hands into his jeans to rub his hard cock.

'Get undressed, Candy,' he orders in a rough voice, and I turn to watch her remove her G-string and undo her bra. She's curvy and soft with voluptuous breasts and I reach out tentatively to touch them. Jackson sits me up and gently pushes me to Candy and guides my mouth onto her breast, and a thrill shoots through me before I greedily grab them and try and fit them into my mouth. Jackson, his cock getting harder, then moves my hands to Candy's wet pussy. I gasp at the thrill of touching her there.

Jackson moves me back to the laying down position with my legs apart, and Candy leans over me so I can continue to suck and lick her nipples. Jackson guides her fingers in and out of my slick pussy, then puts them into her mouth and then my mouth. He has undone his jeans and stands naked beside us, his hard cock straight out.

Candy is on her knees above me and moves her mouth off my

breasts and onto Jackson's cock. I wriggle down until Candy is sitting on my face, longing to taste her. I probe my tongue inside while she sucks Jackson's cock until it's so big he's choking her. Candy is choking and groaning as I bring her closer and closer to orgasm.

Jackson uses all his willpower not to come as he watches my hands on Candy's breasts while Candy moves up and down on my tongue.

With Jackson's cock still in her mouth, Candy comes all over my face and her teeth graze his thick shaft in her ecstasy.

Jackson quickly moves onto the couch behind Candy and fucks her from behind while she kisses me and licks her cum from my face. Jackson fucks her harder and harder, and she screams for more. My brain starts to take over and tears squeeze out of my eyes as I watch Jackson fucking Candy. I'm all mixed up; it feels like a betrayal.

Jackson sees my tears and pulls out, moving Candy away.

'It's your turn, Skye, I'm saving the best for last,' Jackson says as he kisses the tears on my cheeks and softly onto my lips. He moves his mouth to my ear. 'I'm sorry, it doesn't mean anything, I'll never do that again, I promise. It's you I want, it's you I love.'

He moves his cock into my mouth and I can taste Candy on him. I try and block her out, and I know he can feel me wavering. He moves down to taste me, thrusting his tongue inside my swollen lips.

The room sways and it feels like ants are crawling all over my body as he expertly puts the perfect pressure on my clit. I am defenseless when he has his tongue here. All thoughts disappear and I am close to coming like I've never come before. I move my hips up as Jackson licks harder and faster, moving his tongue from my clit to my arse, licking all around it to make it slick and wet while he tells me he's going to fuck it hard. I move my hips higher, wanting more.

'You're so wet Skye, I'm going to fuck you in both places,' he groans as he scoops sticky wetness from my swollen lips and rubs it into my arse before gently pushing a finger in, slowly, while his tongue flicks and licks my clit. He reaches for lube and I shiver at the sensation of the cold liquid as he squeezes it onto my tight hole, pushing his finger in further. I can barely take it. He pushes it in slowly and gently and the intensity of the sensation almost brings me undone.

'Fuck me up the arse,' I whimper, while his finger goes in and out. He pulls his finger out and I move onto my hands and knees so he can spread my cheeks. He gently moves his rock-hard cock into the tight space. Candy scoops up her clothes and starts to leave. She turns and watches as Jackson gently pushes into me and continues to touch my breasts and erect nipples. Jackson goes slowly in and out of my tightness, kissing me on the back of the neck while asking, *you like this?* I'm screaming and my whole body shudders.

'You're so tight,' Jackson says as he pushes in further. 'Push back on me so I can give it to you.'

While he pushes in gently he flicks his fingers on my clit then slides them in and out. 'I'm going to come,' I pant. 'Don't stop. Fuck me harder, make me come.'

Jackson's cock is like a magic wand, and I'm there. I scream *fuck me, now!* and feel him release in my arse. He holds his fingers still inside me as I come apart.

Jackson gently pulls out and I feel the dribble of his sticky wetness. I don't know why or how, but I'm sobbing, overwhelmed by emotion. I roll onto my back, fully spent. Jackson lays on me and kisses my lips, cheeks, and wet eyes.

'You are gorgeous, you are so, so gorgeous,' he whispers as we kiss and hold each other tight, having just shared my most intimate sexual experience. I never imagined how good it would feel to be fucked there, like that.

I have forgotten all about Candy; it's just me and Jackson in this moment.

Candy stands quietly at the door, understanding she's played a role in helping Jackson live out one of his porn movie sexual fantasies but that's all she will ever be – a side part. She will never play the main role, ever. Jackson has eyes only for Skye, and Skye only.

9

SKYE

It is a Sunday afternoon and my car is packed with seedlings for Quinton. Mum is in the garden and I'm fussing around like a Kelpie with new pups.

'My goodness girl,' Bev says as she pulls out weeds that have sprung up in her flourishing corn crop. 'You're more nervous than a long-tailed cat in a room full of rocking chairs.'

'I'm not nervous, Mum. I'm just excited to start a new garden and show Quinton some of the things that you've been showing me since I was three years old. He's going to love it. He's so into that sort of stuff. I haven't met anyone like him before.'

Bev raises her eyebrows.

'Am I sensing something more going on here?'

'No Bev, of course not. We just have a common interest in things like soil, that sort of stuff.'

'As long as that's all it is,' Bev says, eyeing my outfit. Loose Katherine Hepburn casual navy pants and an oversized white collared shirt, accompanied by my favourite wide-brimmed navy bucket hat and oversized dark-framed sunglasses. I have tamed my long hair into a single braid which snakes down my back.

'I don't want my girl going and wrecking any relationships. With that beautiful body of yours and that pretty face, you could be biting off more than you can chew.'

If only she knew.

'Haha, that is the last thing in my mind, and as you know, Jackson's my guy,' I say.

Bev rolls her eyes. 'Jackson, hmmm. Waltzes in trying to impress you with all his money and his fancy cars and new house. He's all show, you know that, don't you?'

'Maybe. It's a good show to be part of though!' Noticing Mum's pursed lips I shift off the topic of Jackson.

'I'm just going over there with some of our seedlings to help him get Susan's garden back in shape. Do you know how many hours I spent in that garden? People around town say her veggies were almost as good as yours.'

'Not as good as mine though?'

'Never as good as yours, Mum. I reckon we should do away with some of the lawn and trees and put more garden beds in and set up a business to sell your veggies. People want to eat fresh, from the gate to the plate.'

Mum stands up to stretch and I hear her knees creak. 'Getting harder to get up these days. Not sure if I have it in me.'

'I'll help, I've still got plenty of stretch in these knees,' I say, squatting down to pull some weeds for her. 'It's a good way to earn a bit of extra cash. You never know, you might want to put it towards a cruise ship holiday, for you and Bill.'

'Maybe,' Bev says. 'I do enjoy growing the veggies.'

'No shit Sherlock. You love it!'

We collapse into giggles. Mum helps me up from the ground and we end up in our usual hug. Mum's always been a hugger; I love that about her.

'I'd better go. Time to help someone else get their garden started. I shouldn't be home too late.'

'Okay love, if I'm not here, don't worry. I'm going down to the club for the cash draw, try and win myself some easy money. Not much chance of winning, but you've got to be in it to win it, and I'd hate to not be there and have my name called out.'

'True, and if my name gets called out I don't want to know! But if I get finished in time, I'll meet you there, otherwise I'll just see you back at home.'

'Well, after the club I was planning to go round to Bill's to watch a movie or something.'

'Oh, I see. Or something,' I tease.

'Not that sort of something, we're just friends. I've told you that before.'

I pull her straw gardening hat down onto her head. As I drive off, I watch her wave to me until I turn the corner. With tears in my eyes, I wonder how I'd ever live without her. Admonishing myself for being a sentimental fool, I focus forward to the task at hand. A simple gardening session. Nothing less, nothing more.

...

QUINTON IS ALREADY in the garden when I arrive. It is a warm, sunny day with a breeze that keeps the temperature in the full blazing sun more bearable.

'Started without me?' I say, standing over him with two trays of seedlings. Quinton stands, lifts his cowboy hat off his head and wipes his sweaty forehead with his hanky.

'I wanted to be ready when you came,' he says with a broad grin.

I admire his strong arms and muscles in a collared shirt that he's ripped the sleeves out of. His trademark jeans hug every perfectly-proportioned body part from the waist down.

'Aren't you hot in those jeans?' I ask. *Hot alright.*

'No, not especially. I'm used to wearing jeans all year round. Shorts are no good when you're out on a motorbike so I don't notice it. Plus, it's not half as hot here as what it is out west.'

'I bet it isn't. I think today's only going to be mid-twenties.'

'That's practically cold, I should go in and get myself a jumper,' he says with a wink.

He walks with me to the car to unpack the seedlings and bags of home-grown soil from the large buckets in the back corner of our yard. I chatter away, explaining how we make our soil while showing him around his garden shed, pointing out the different buckets and bins Susan and I used to potter around in.

'You sure do know your way around,' Quinton comments.

'I love this garden. Susan spent so much time making it beautiful. It was a real shame when she left and it all just went to waste,' I say. 'I really wanted to try and keep it going when they were trying to sell. She was ready to retire before Fred, so she left the farm and spent all her time on the Gold Coast looking for a new place before it was sold. Every day I'd come to work and see the garden wilting and dying. But it wasn't really my business to interfere.'

'Do you still see Susan and Fred?' Quinton asks, as we kneel in the garden bed to start planting corn.

'Susan and Mum are good friends, and whenever she's back in town for anything she always pops around for a cuppa. I don't actually see her that much because it's usually when I'm at work.'

'Beth and I have told Austin that Susan and Fred are welcome out here anytime,' Quinton says.

'Why doesn't that surprise me? You're so nice, not many people would think of that.'

'We're grateful to have Austin stay on, the least we can do is invite his parents out. But they haven't come.' Quinton moves along to the next row and I move with him, showing him how to space out the bean seedlings so they can grow up the trellises which had stood bare since Susan left.

'Susan used to be a model and being on the Gold Coast, I'd say she could probably get back into it. She's really beautiful, she's got so much style.'

'You could be a model,' Quinton says, methodically moving along the bean row.

'Me? A model? I don't think so.'

Quinton's voice goes husky.

'You're pretty enough, and your body...' I look up from the garden to see him blushing. I blush too.

'Thank you, that's very nice of you to say. But no, being a model has never interested me. I'm happy in Scone, working out here, living with Mum, doing things in the community, being in the garden, growing a few veggies, competing in a few triathlons here and there. I'm very, very content.'

Simultaneously we both sit up on our knees and look at each other.

'It's nice to hear that you like it here. It is a good community?'

'It's a great community. Maybe you could join the football club?'

'I used to play a bit of football at school, but I haven't played for a while. I'm probably not fit enough.'

'You'll be fit enough for the Scone Thoroughbreds. They're always keen for new players, they're one of the best country rugby league clubs around. Next season you should definitely play, but what you should do before that is train for it.'

'How do you train for footy? I've never trained a day in my life,' Quinton says.

'I'll teach you how to train. I've been training since I was fifteen.'

'Really? Okay then, you're on,' Quinton says as he stands and dusts off his hands. 'Want a drink?'

'Yeah, that'd be good.' I stand as well, admiring the rows of neatly planted seedlings while I try and swallow the anger that bubbles inside at the thought of how lonely Quinton must be. How stupid is Beth not to realise this? It is fine for her, she's never here long enough to settle in or get lonely. Quinton has no friends or family around him, and all he does is work.

I eventually join him on the back verandah where he sits with his legs dangling over the side.

He hands me a glass of Cottee's fruit cup cordial. 'I haven't really got biscuits or anything to offer you.'

'I'm not hungry, I had a big breakfast.' I crouch down next to him, losing my balance and falling onto his lap.

'Sorry,' I apologise as I regain my balance while trying not to spill my drink. I do save it but end up sitting closer than intended, our legs touching. I wonder if he can feel the heat burning into his leg like I can.

'What do I owe you and your Mum for all those seedlings?'

'Nothing, nothing at all! We have so many,' I say.

'I don't expect you to give them to me. You should be selling them, not giving them away. You could make a little side business out of it.'

'Funny you should say that. I was just talking to Mum about setting up a more dedicated vegetable stall at the markets or something. We grow more than what we can eat, and we also give away a lot to our friends and donate to the Salvos who run a soup kitchen of sorts, and we still have some left. There would be a lot of people out there who'd love fresh veggies every week.'

'You should, definitely. Just thinking about what we've planted today, I'm pretty sure I won't be able to eat it all so you could have some for your market stall from here.'

My mind ticks over – with the size of Quinton and Beth's garden and extra beds in our garden, we could set up a big stall at the markets. We might also be able to expand the soup kitchen and turn it into some sort of food pantry, so people who are struggling to put good food on the table have access to fresh vegetables.

'Maybe it's a sign, a little side project for us all,' I say. 'Mum works a few jobs to make ends meet, but they're all indoors and she hates being inside. This might be a way for her to spend more time in her favourite place, her garden.'

'It gives me something to do as well,' Quinton says. 'I'm always looking for an outdoor project, the days can get long when Beth's away.'

I jump off the verandah before I give away my true feelings about Beth being away so much and start walking towards the gate.

'Hey, where are you going?'

'I need to go to the loo.'

'Go in the house.'

'I don't want to impose.'

'You're not imposing. It's just a toilet and it's much closer.'

I feel awkward going into Quinton and Beth's home, even though I've spent a lot of time in it over the years and know the layout intimately.

I remove my gardening boots at the door and hang my hat on the hook. Quinton is trying to explain where the toilet is but I'm already heading in the right direction.

'Right,' he says as he follows me inside. 'You know your way around already.'

I am busting by the time I get to the toilet and as I roughly pull my pants off something falls out of the pocket and onto the floor. It's a condom from the last time I was with Jackson. He is slack with using them and although I have just booked into the doctor for an IUD, that's not until next month, and the last thing I want is to get pregnant.

I shove it back into my pocket, pushing any thoughts of Jackson aside. He is the last person on my mind after spending the past couple of hours with my dream cowboy who gets dreamier with every moment.

'Stop it,' I whisper to the girl in the mirror whose braid is coming loose after being under a hat. 'Quinton is not yours to dream about. Pull yourself together and go home!'

When I return, he's waiting in the kitchen, and I continue the conversation from where it left off, my nervous chatter hiding my embarrassment at carrying a condom around in my pocket.

'I used to hang out a lot with Susan, from when I was quite young,' I say as I rinse our glasses in the sink, dry and return them to the cupboard.

'Her and Mum have always had the common interest with the gardening and Susan was always hosting garden parties. I spent as much time here as I did at home growing up. That's how I got the job in the first place. I was always helping in the shed, and they offered me a job when I turned sixteen because I was saving up for my first car.'

Quinton is leaning against the bench, watching me easily navigate my way around his kitchen.

'You bought your first car yourself?'

'Yeah, it's always just been Mum and me and we've never had much spare cash laying around.'

'What happened to your dad?'

'I never knew him. He cleared out when I was young.'

'I'm sorry,' Quinton says, 'I can't imagine.'

'No need to be sorry. Makes no difference to me. I've got the best Mum in the world.'

'I've got a nice Mum too, and Dad,' Quinton says. 'But I left home when I was young, twelve, to go to boarding school, and that made me grow up quickly.'

I lean down into the cupboard under the sink to put the washing up brush away, not realising a couple of my top buttons have come loose. Quinton stops mid-sentence and I catch him looking straight down my shirt.

I stand quickly and go to do the buttons up, but he moves forward to stop me.

'Leave them,' he says quietly. I can smell the sweat on his skin and a faint layer of his warm spice deodorant.

I slowly undo the buttons on my shirt to reveal my naked breasts.

'You're not wearing a bra,' Quinton says. 'You don't mean to tell me I have been in close proximity to you all this time without knowing you were...'

'Naked?' I suggest.

I notice his Adam's apple move as he swallows.

'I never wear a bra when I'm gardening. I can't stand being confined when I'm hot and sweating and I don't need a bra in the garden because it's not like when I go for a run. I can just hang loose.'

I'm rambling. Quinton raises one of his dark eyebrows, gently reaching out to touch one of my nipples, sending a thrill of anticipation through me that makes my legs shake.

I stand perfectly still while he leans in to kiss me, pulling out my long plait until my hair is loose while his lips are on mine, sending butterflies from my stomach to my toes.

'Have you got any idea how hard it's been to avoid you since that day in the tearoom? Since tasting you and having you let it all go in my mouth?' He groans into my mouth while threading his fingers through my hair.

I snap, returning his kiss passionately and falling into him, yearning to feel his skin on mine.

'I've wanted you just as badly back,' I say breathlessly inbetween desperate, needy kisses. 'Not a minute goes by that I don't think about you and imagine what it felt like to have you all over my body, on me, under me, making me come with your tongue.'

We grab at each other as I lift his sleeveless shirt over his head, running my hands up and down his muscly back and melting at the feel of his soft, smooth skin.

'I feel like coming every time I look at you,' I say, running my fingers gently over his rock hard chest.

'These arms.' I kiss his bicep on one side, then the other.

'This chin.' I kiss his chin.

'These lips.' I kiss them softly, gently then harder, my tongue probing. I move one hand down to feel what I know will be there.

'This hard cock.'

Quinton tangles his fingers in my hair and pulls me to him roughly. 'How many times have you thought of me since that day?' he asks.

'So many times.'

He moves his mouth to my ear and his hot breath sends shivers to the tips of my toes. 'And how many times have you made yourself come thinking of me,' he whispers, and I feel his cock grow bigger and harder.

I undo his jeans and quickly push them to the ground, admiring the way he is tenting his boxer shorts. I whisper in his ear as I rest my hand gently on his waist. 'How badly do you want me to touch it?'

He answers by pulling my hair tighter. I move my hand down and feel it grow bigger, before moving it away, teasing him.

'You're going to have to wait.' I step back and with my fingertips I circle my erect nipples while he watches.

I undo my pants and slowly push them down to reveal my lacy black G-string.

'You mean to tell me, not only did you have no bra while I knelt next to you in the garden, but you're wearing that?'

Quinton leans down to put one breast in his mouth, then the other, before scooping me up with one arm and carrying me effortlessly to the spare bedroom.

He sits me on the edge of the bed and kneels so he can ravage my breasts, pushing my shirt off. I arch my back as he licks and sucks. He pushes me roughly back onto the bed. I watch him take off his boxers, and he's pointing straight at me, begging for my mouth.

He climbs onto me and I wriggle down so I can reach what I'm crying out for. 'I want you to fill my mouth, let me suck it, I want it.'

I greedily grab for him. He only lets me have it for the briefest moment and I groan in protest as he pulls out of my mouth and flips onto his back.

'Sit on my face, now,' he orders in a low growl that sends lightning bolts to my toes. I lower myself onto his tongue and he pushes my G-string aside before reaching his hands up to encircle my breasts. His tongue goes in deep while he rubs his rough fingers over my nipples. The G-string is restricting him; having to move off his tongue for a brief moment to take it off nearly kills me. Back on his face, with his tongue where I want it, feels so damn good. He nibbles, bites, sucks and flicks his tongue over and around my clit until I can't feel my bones.

He pushes me up and I want to beg for more, but before I can get any words out he has a finger inside me and his mouth back on my clit. It's too much, I can't control myself and I'm there, a flash of light, heat and tremble all at once.

I shudder and grip his finger as I cover his face in my sweet stickiness. Panting, I go to climb off but he holds me there and keeps moving his tongue over my pulsing clit. I can hardly bear it.

'You need more. I know it.' There's that low growl again.

'Oh Quinton, Quinton,' I pant as he thrusts his tongue in again and again. I reach back to feel his shaft, which is even harder than when I had it in my mouth.

I want his cock back in my mouth but I can't move. I pant as he holds me on his face. Eventually he lets me go. 'You can only have it if I can still have it,' he instructs, turning me around so I am still on his face while I swallow him whole.

We are both breathing heavily, sweating and hot. I moan onto his cock, urging him to come in my mouth while he urges me to come in his.

Quinton loses control first and I pull and swallow and refuse to let him out until he's fully spent and goes slack. When he's done I turn back around, guiding his fingers into me as I lean down to kiss him, his cum coating the inside of my mouth and my lips.

He kisses me deeply while his fingers slide in and out. I kneel beside him and he watches my fingers circle my clit while his fingers move in and out quickly.

'Quinton, Quinton, more, I want more. I'm coming, I'm coming.' I call out loudly as I orgasm for the second time and collapse onto his chest in a pool of sweat.

He wraps his arms around me and hugs me tight, my ear right on his beating heart. I lay listening to his heartbeat gradually slow down until eventually returning to a normal rhythm and we fall into a deep, satisfied sleep.

····

WE WAKE at the same time, still snuggled close, and for a few seconds I wonder if life can get any better. While I am in Quinton's arms, it is easy to chase away any thoughts of Beth, Jackson – anyone for that matter. It is just Quinton and I, in our love bubble. Nothing and nobody else matters.

'Hello, you,' he says as he kisses me on the forehead.

'Hello you. What time is it?'

'Who cares what time it is?'

'What about the pigs?'

'Who cares about the pigs?' Quinton says as he explores my body.

'We have to care about the pigs, Quinton.'

'Fine. On one condition.' He rolls me over and holds me around the waist, kissing me in the middle of my back. 'What's that?'

'When we finish the pigs, you'll come back. We have unfinished business.'

'And what might that be?'

He puts his mouth to my ear. 'I want all of you, every bit.'

Goosebumps run down my arms, making my hairs stand on end.

'Your wish is my command.'

'You want food first?' he asks.

'You are my food. You're all the food I need.'

I turn around and kiss him for the longest time and we're within moments of not being able to get out of bed.

Reluctantly, Quinton sits up to get ready for work. I pull him back. As much as I have loved all our foreplay, I need more of him, all of him. It suddenly feels urgent to have him inside me.

'I want you, all day and all night,' I say, about to profess complete and total adoration.

The shrill and intruding sound of the telephone from the kitchen interrupts me.

'Don't answer it,' I urge, as I sit on him and move my hands over his chest.

Quinton pushes me gently away.

'I've got a problem ignoring the phone, just in case it's something important. It could be Mum or Dad or, someone else...'

My stomach lurches. Someone else. Someone like Beth. I swallow my guilt as he jogs, naked, to the kitchen.

'Hello,' I hear him say. 'What? Is she...' I strain to hear his words, as I try and ascertain if he's in a panic or if it's just a work call. To distract myself I go to the bathroom and clean myself up. I find my shirt but can't find my G-string. Still distracted, I find my pants and fumble to pull them on, not realising the condom falls out and slips under the edge of the bed.

He is still on the phone when I get to the kitchen, listening intently. When he sees me, he turns his back and quickly wraps up the call.

His demeanor is completely changed and he can't look me in the eye.

'Everything okay?' I ask with concern.

'Yeah, actually no, I'm not sure it is.'

'What is it?'

Quinton's face turns red and he folds his arms across his chest.

'It was Beth's Mum,' he says, his voice shaking.

My stomach lurches again and I cross my arms to protect myself from whatever is coming next.

'What did she want?' I try and act concerned, although I don't want to know.

'Beth's been in an accident. She's in the hospital.'

I feel physically sick. I'm such a bitch. What have I done?

'Is it bad?'

'Yes, it's bad.'

A long, excruciating silence stretches between us.

'I've got to go to Sydney,' he says, his arms still crossed.

'Okay. Okay. I'll get out of your hair.'

I hesitate, wondering if I should hug him. I decide not to. He looks relieved.

I grab my shoes clumsily on my way out, pulling them on as I run to the car, holding in my tears until I am safely inside.

As soon as I close the door the sobs come. Hiccupping and crying with an aching heart, I wonder how things could go from where they were to where they are.

10

SKYE

C andy knocks lightly on the door, and it only takes a few seconds for Bev to answer.

'Where is she?'

'On the couch,' Bev whispers.

'How long has she been there?'

'Days. She won't tell me what's happened but she hasn't left the house. She didn't want me to call you but I'm at my wit's end.'

Candy pushes past. 'I've got this.' She winks at Bev with her twinkling crystal blue eyes. Her short, blonde wavy hair frames perfectly her round face, as though she's just walked out of a hairdressing salon (which she has). She wiggles her beautifully-generous hips and marches into the dark lounge room.

Candy opens the curtains wide, letting the sunlight stream across the lump on the couch underneath a blanket.

'Shut the curtains,' I groan.

'No, I will not. It's a beautiful day outside. It's about time you got off the couch and stopped feeling sorry for yourself.'

I pull the blanket further over my head.

'No.'

Candy pulls the rug off and kneels down next to me, landing a sloppy kiss on my cheek.

'Eeeww,' I say, opening one bloodshot and puffy eye, then the other.

'What happened?' Candy asks.

'Nothing. I'm just having a few down days.'

'Bullshit. Something's happened. This is not the Skye we know. The Skye we know doesn't spend days on the couch, refusing to speak to her best friend in the whole world, refusing to let her Mum open the curtains and let the sunlight in.'

I sit up, slowly, my shoulders slumped.

'I'm an idiot.'

'We all know that!' Candy laughs, pushing me against the shoulder as she sits down next to me. Candy wraps her arms around me and she's like hugging a big comfy pillow.

'You smell nice,' I say.

'You don't. How long since you've had a shower? My goodness girl, look at your hair. You could fry chips in it!' I roll my eyes.

'Skedaddle,' Candy pushes me off the couch and gives me a friendly kick up the bum. 'Get that stringy hair and those smelly underarms into the shower.'

Half an hour later, I pat into our small, cosy, country kitchen, dressed in denim cut-off shorts and a plain black T-shirt, my damp, dark hair tumbling around my shoulders.

It is a familiar kitchen scene. Bev at the stove flipping a batch of pancakes, and Candy cutting strawberries into perfectly neat slices and arranging them on a plate.

'Smells good,' I murmur, famished.

Candy orders me to sit with her eyes and plants a large steaming cup of coffee on our sage formica table. I ease myself into a matching sage leather chair with silver stud detail and white plastic socks to stop it from scratching our polished timber floor.

The feel of the smooth thick rim of my favourite home-made deep pink and blue pottery mug on my lips is as soothing as aloe vera gel on sunburn. Mum and I found the mug at a roadhouse between here and Armidale on a special holiday when I was a teenager. It is one of my favourite holidays, where we slept in the back of the station wagon and discovered an immeasurable number of special bush tracks and waterfalls off the beaten track.

I liberally cover my heaped plate of pancakes with maple syrup and arrange Candy's neat strawberries on top.

'You want cream, love?' Mum says from the fridge, which still has some of my pre-school artwork with curled edges held in place by an eclectic collection of magnets. From a set of matching green plastic frogs with various expressions to ceramic cottages and farm animals from the discount store Clint's Crazy Bargains.

'That is a stupid question, Mum.'

The three of us eat and joked around the square table with skinny stork-like legs we have been sitting around since Candy and I were in primary school.

'Your pancakes are next level, Mum,' I say, hungrily shoveling soft pillows with the perfect butter crunch edges into my mouth. I look up to catch her intent gaze.

'Stop fussing,' I lecture. 'I'm fine, as you can see. All I needed was a shower and a plate of your pancakes.'

'I'm not fussing,' she says. 'I've got to head off, my shift at the club starts soon.' She breathes in the apple scent of my freshly washed hair as she kisses me on the top of the head.

'Where's mine?' Candy protests.

Mum kisses the top of her head with a smile. 'See you later girls, there's plenty of mixture left in the fridge if you want more.'

'Do you realise you're the sole reason my hips jiggle like they do?' Candy groans, as she takes another mouthful.

Candy waits until she hears Mum's car back out of the driveway.

'Okay girl, spill. I want to know everything. Don't leave out any details. Start to finish.'

I sigh, the thought of Quinton sitting beside Beth's hospital bed still giving me heart palpations in a mix of guilt, shame and desire.

'You know how I was telling you about my hot boss?'

'You mean the cowboy?'

'Yes, the cowboy.'

'Of course I do. I can't wait to lay eyes on this man. I thought for sure he'd be in for a haircut by now.'

'You won't be meeting him,' I say. 'And if he comes in for a haircut you need to tell him you are booked out. I can never face him, ever again.'

'Um, how is that going to work? Isn't he your employer?'

My face reddens. 'Yes, but I honestly don't think I can ever go to work again.'

'That's ridiculous Skye, you have to go to work! It can't be that bad, surely.'

'It is. Worse.'

I take a deep breath. 'As you know, he's moved here with his girl-friend, Beth, a lawyer in Sydney. She comes and goes but one day not too long ago when she left he was really upset...'

Candy rolls her eyes. 'Let me guess, and you just happened to be there to comfort him?'

'It wasn't like that, at all. You make me sound so slutty.'

Candy raises an eyebrow. 'That's not what I mean. Haven't I taught you anything? Rebound sex can be good sex, but only if you don't get involved. And it's pretty obvious you made the fatal mistake of getting involved.'

'Firstly, we didn't have sex. It was nothing like that, things just sort of happened, really naturally. He was really into it, and then he wasn't, and then he was really embarrassed, and he was so adorable and sweet, and it just made me want him even more. And I'll have you know, thank you very much, that I do listen to you and I one hundred percent know rebound sex is sex with no future.'

'If that's the case, what is going on? I've not seen you like this since Jackson left for the first time and told you he thought it would be better if you broke up rather than sit home and pine for him. He was right, but you still pined.'

I roll my eyes. I did pine. Jackson had been my first love, or so I thought.

'I gave him his space, and we got back to work, just as friends, as if nothing had ever happened,' I continue softly. 'If what you're telling me is correct, why did you end up on the couch for three days in a depression? This cowboy must be something serious to put you in a spiral like that?'

'Oh Candy,' I gasp. 'He is the most gorgeous, hottest, loveliest, hottest man I have ever met. I didn't think it was possible for a man to be as perfect as him.'

'He's got you good for someone you said was just a friend,' Candy comments.

I sigh. 'I know. We were, are, oh Candy, it's such a mess! I thought we could just be friends so Mum and I gave him some vegetable seedlings for the garden, you know, the big garden I used to help Susan with all the time that's gone to rack and ruin, and he is lonely because I have no idea where Beth is.'

'Here we go,' Candy laughs, and tucks a strand of my hair behind my ear. 'Don't tell me you had dirty, filthy garden sex.'

We burst into giggles. 'No, I did not. But somehow over the course of the afternoon we ended up in the house and then the bedroom...'

'You mean the bedroom he sleeps in with Beth?' Candy's eyes are wide.

'No, not the main bedroom, the spare bedroom. It looked like he'd been sleeping in there though, and it was so easy to forget Beth even exists because at that moment it was all about me and Quinton.'

Candy raises an eyebrow.

'I know, I know. You've told me so many times, *never have an affair with a made guy.*'

'Yet, here you are. What I don't understand yet is why you have just spent days on the couch unable to face the day? Is it guilt?'

'No, it's not that. Quinton is amazing. So fucking hot, I tell you what. I have never ever, ever...' I blush.

'Hotter than Jackson?' Candy's eyes are wide and I know she's desperate for details I'm never going to share.

'So much hotter than Jackson. I mean, Jackson's hot. Of course.' Candy and I look away at the same time.

'I thought you were back with Jackson,' Candy says.

'I am, well, sort of, not really. It's the same as it always is. As soon as he's gone I won't hear from him until he hits town again. With Jackson it's, casual. Quinton feels so much more real.'

'What is it that makes Quinton so different to any other bloke?' Candy asks, challenging me like she always does to be honest with myself. I don't take the bait; I have no intention of going deep with her while I'm feeling so fragile.

'It's his muscly arms, broad shoulders and cowboy hat, that's what,' I smile wickedly.

Candy squeals.

'He's a real proper cowboy? Seriously, not a pretend cowboy like all the cowboys we know? *Take me to a rodeo so I can save a horse and ride a cowboy* cowboy?'

'That's the one. A real cowboy. True dinks. You know that cowboy you met at the Scone rodeo when we were nineteen, the one with the jet black hair, black hat, red shirt and massive belt buckle?'

'You mean the one with the biggest dick I've ever had in me?' Candy giggles.

'Yes, that's the one, what was his name again? Randy?'

We erupt into hysterics.

'Yes! Randy, and fuck, he sure was randy!' Candy sighs. 'I could have fucked that cowboy until the end of my days but when I woke up the next morning, he'd saddled his horse and ridden away. Bloody cowboys.'

We sigh simultaneously while remembering old times.

'Anyway, Randy was close to being a real cowboy, you'd have to say. But think of someone who's about fifty per cent hotter, is as interested in your mind as he is in your body, probably a whole lot smarter than Randy, who wouldn't ditch you the next morning, and you have Quinton.

We sit in silence for a moment. 'If he's so perfect, what's upset you so much?' Candy asks.

'While we were in the bedroom the phone rang.'

'Don't tell me he answered the phone, what is with that?'

'Yes, he is that kind of guy. The kind who worries that the phone call might be important, so no matter what he's doing he answers it.'

Candy rolls her eyes. 'That's a strike against him.'

'It sure is. I stayed in the bedroom waiting for him to come back but he didn't come back.'

Tears sting my eyes at the memory of the look on his face when I walked into the kitchen. The way he looked through me, closed off.

'Was it Beth on the phone?' Candy reaches over to hold my hand, seeing my distress.

'No, her Mum. Beth's been in an accident, she's in the hospital in Sydney. That's all I know. I got out of there as quickly as I could. He couldn't wait to see the back of me.'

Candy squeezes my hand. 'I'm so sorry, that must have been awkward.'

'I feel like a horrible person plus an absolute idiot for going near this guy who is obviously very much taken and by the look of some of the photos around the house, they've been together for a long time, and I had no business being in his business.'

Candy's eyes flashed. 'Stop that! More like he had no business being in your business. You're too trusting and gullible, he's just used you to fill a gap when he's feeling lonely, and he should have kept his hands to himself!'

'I know, I know, but he's so nice and kind and lovely and a real gentleman. We have this attraction, it's real, I haven't imagined it. There is something magnetic between us.'

'Are you sure you're not living out your fantasy about cowboys? Who you have been obsessed with since you and I went to our first rodeo when we were sixteen years old, giggly school girls dressed up in our cowboy boots, tight jeans and skimpy little tops thinking we were going to get ourselves a cowboy boyfriend when, in actual fact, it was hot and dusty and we were far too young for anyone there?'

'You're probably right,' I say, getting up to rinse out my cup and clear the plates.

'I'm just really hurt and heartbroken, so heartbroken. I don't understand why, when there's really nothing to get that heartbroken over, but he has broken my heart.'

Candy gives me another big, squishy hug.

'Let's go to a rodeo,' Candy jumps up and down in her seat.

'Yes, let's!'

'My precious dear Skye,' she continues. 'While we wait for a rodeo to come to town, what you need is a night out. You and I, this Friday night, are going out to the pub and we are going to partay!!'

I laugh again.

'It's a date!'

'But before we do, let me do something with this boring hair of yours. It needs a trim and maybe a colour.'

'My hair is fine,' I protest.

'Wouldn't you like a few highlights around here, framing your face?'

'No, you are not putting colour in my hair. It doesn't need it. You can blow dry it and maybe cut a bit more off than I've let you in the past but no colouring.'

Candy is running her fingers through my hair, imagining how she would style it if I let her free-range.

'One day I'll get my hands on this beautiful, luxurious hair of yours.'

'Maybe, maybe not. For now, you're going to have to save all your experimenting for your own hair. You can get away with it, I can't. It doesn't matter what style or what colour, you always look like you're straight out of *Cleo* magazine.'

'Why thank you lovely lady, you're a keeper.' Candy tips her head to the side and gives me her best model pose.

We erupt into laughter, and just like that, all is well with my world again.

11

QUINTON

I wait until everyone else has left before I pull Skye aside.

Since returning from Sydney where Beth is in intensive care after a car accident which almost killed her, I've avoided Skye. Likewise, she's given me the space she knows I need.

I have made the decision to commit to Beth. I can see in Skye's eyes that she knows this before I tell her. We are outside, under the shade of a maple tree. The way the dappled late afternoon light falls onto her face gives it an ethereal glow, making it hard for me to look away, and even harder to say what I'm about to say.

'I'm really sorry, Skye. I. Shouldn't. Have...' I start, haltingly.

'You shouldn't have what?' she probes. I flush bright red and look at my feet.

'I shouldn't have led you on like that. I shouldn't have been with you in that way.'

'You didn't lead me on. You did what you wanted. What I wanted. What we both wanted.'

I look up, and she has me locked in a piercing gaze. 'It was what you wanted, I know you wanted it. What we did wasn't an act.'

I turn away in shame. What is it about this girl? She can read me like a book, and she isn't going to let me shy away from what was between us.

I slowly lift my chin and move my eyes to meet hers.

'You're right. Yes, it is what I wanted, at the time. It was real, and I meant everything I said, and I did. But I can't do any of that ever again. I'm fully committed to Beth. She and I have been together for a really long time, and we have a whole future ahead of us. I need to dedicate myself to the life we have planned.'

I falter as I see her large brown eyes fill with tears.

'I'm really sorry, Skye, but there's no future between us.'

A giant tear rolls over the long, dark lashes of one of her bottom eyelids and slowly down her cheek.

'I don't believe this is what you want, Quinton, but I'm also not going to play second fiddle to anyone or be your backup plan or second best. If it's reality you really want, then it's reality you should have. The reality is, you can't have us both. If you choose Beth, then that's that.'

My mind is spinning out of control. I had this conversation rehearsed so clearly in my mind. It was going to be cut and dry, straightforward, and now all I want to do was lift this young, hot, gorgeous girl into my arms, have her wrap her legs around me and finish what we'd started.

Skye knows I'm weakening. But the image of Beth laying in that hospital bed and knowing how close I was to losing her was a reality check. Beth is my first love and so far, we have stood the test of time. We've known each other since she was in university and in those exciting, non-stop party years we shared our dreams and made them come true, together.

'You don't make it easy on a bloke, do you?'

She smiles, its dazzling.

'I can't help the way I feel, Quinton. From the moment I first laid eyes on you, I fell instantly, madly, deeply in love.'

'How can that be?' I ask. 'You hardly even know me.'

'I know you enough,' she replies, tears running unchecked down her cheeks. 'I know what you like. I know what you don't like. I know you're a good person, and I also know...' she moves closer, 'you are all the man I'll ever want and need.'

I take a step back, my willpower faltering.

'Um, there's something else I wanted to say. It's about when Beth comes home. She's going to need me to look after her for a while, and I, ah, am not sure how it will be with you working here.'

Skye's shoulders stiffen and she wipes her eyes.

'What are you saying? Are you sacking me?'

'No, no, I'm not. I'm not trying to sack you. There is absolutely nothing wrong with the quality and the standard of your work, and I couldn't run this place without you. Your experience and knowledge is highly valued.'

Skye rolls her eyes.

'Cut the bullshit, Quinton.'

I blunder on. 'It's just that when Beth's here, I don't think I could be in the same room as the two of you together and hide what's happened. It will feel, I don't know. Wrong. Really wrong.'

'That's fine. It *will* feel wrong, especially if you keep me a secret from Beth, which I'm assuming is part of your plan? You never want her to know, right? You want to just sweep me under the rug and pretend that what happened between us never happened?

I shrug my shoulders, unable to answer.

'It's becoming clearer,' she says, eyes blazing. 'You do realise you're going to have to be stronger than that. You need to make a decision and stick with it, and if you choose Beth, then your eyes should only be for her and when you look at me, you need to not look at me that way. You can't have us both.'

'I know I can't have you both, that's what I'm trying to say,' I reply, frustration creeping in. 'You've got me all in a tangle, Skye. I want to be honest, I want to be really honest with you. I don't want to hide anything from you.'

'So does this mean you are going to be honest with Beth too?'

I flush again.

'No, no, I haven't, I couldn't. She is in the hospital, and she is badly hurt. I don't want to put that on her until she is better. And you and me, it's nothing. It doesn't mean anything. It is just a physical attraction.'

Skye's eyes widen and I see her hands form into fists.

'How could you say I don't mean anything?'

'That's not what I meant, I just meant that you and I, it's just a physical thing, that's all. Stop trying to mess with my head.'

Skye's voice gets louder. 'It meant a whole lot and you know it.' She stares at me, her chin out, for several excruciatingly long seconds, uncurls her fists and her shoulders slump.

'This conversation isn't getting either of us anywhere,' she says softly. 'As much as I care for you, I have enough self-esteem to know I'm not going to play second fiddle to Beth.'

I don't reply, I have run out of words.

'I'd better go, Mum's cooking dinner and we're having friends over tonight.' She turns away and takes a few steps before turning back. 'Honestly, Quinton, I wish you and Beth all the best, and I'm going to make it easy for you. As soon as I can find another job, I'll stop coming out here. That way you can make a fresh start, and I can make a fresh start. Whatever happened between us will stay between us. Our secret is safe with me.'

I breathe a sigh of relief.

'Thankyou, Skye, once again, I'm sorry. I didn't set out to intentionally hurt you.'

'I know you didn't.'

Mustering the small amount of dignity she has left, Skye walks to her car without looking back. If she had, she would have seen me torn into pieces about what was right and what was wrong. Beth was right, said my head but my body, and my heart, weren't going to be able to let Skye go quite that easily.

12

SKYE

I wander around Jackson's house straightening things after his departure, still sore from the amount of times I'd made him fuck me up the arse while he was home. I used him to obliterate Quinton, to bring myself back to Jackson, the man I thought I would love forever before my dream man in a cowboy hat and tight jeans walked into my life.

I stayed at his house the whole time he was home on leave, spending every spare moment naked, licking, sucking and making new, exciting, wild memories with Jackson.

'How about you move into my place and look after it while I'm not here?' he'd said on our final night.

'I wouldn't expect to live here without paying rent,' I replied.

'You've just paid your rent, but maybe I'll collect a bit more.' He rolled me onto my side so he could play with my arse cheeks before spreading them apart and fucking me from behind one more time.

As much as I didn't want to leave the safety and familiarity of what I was used to, just Mum and I, maybe it was time to give Bev her own space.

And that is how I ended up here, in this beautiful historic homestead-style house with an all the way round bull-nosed verandah and sprawling cottage gardens begging to be brought back to life.

I am a grown-up now, keeping house for my long-distance boyfriend. Ready to start my happily ever after.

13

SKYE

'Skye!' Candy calls enthusiastically from the back of the salon where she is putting rollers into the short, thinning hair one of her elderly regulars, Nancy, who comes in once a week for a wash, a curl and a blow dry. A widow in her eighties, Nancy has trouble lifting her arms above her shoulders to do her own hair. Her weekly visit also catches her up on what's happening in town, and keeps her connected.

I'm carrying a tray of freshly baked muffins, raspberry and white chocolate. I baked them after Jackson left for an important meeting which he mentioned might be his ticket to move home permanently.

Cooking and gardening are my equalisers, helping me get back into balance after the strange feelings living in Jackson's house, and even stranger feelings of where I would go if he moved home permanently.

'Good morning, girls,' I say cheerfully, 'thought you might need some morning tea.'

'You shouldn't have, Candy says, patting her stomach, wondering how many more of Skye's endless supply of home-baked goods her short, round figure could cater for. 'My favourite,' she says as I lift the tea towel to show her what is underneath.

'There's more than enough for you, too, Nancy,' I say. Nancy smiles in reply.

'She is as deaf as a post and hasn't heard a word,' Candy says as she completes the last roller. 'I'm just about to put the dryer on. You love a little nap under the dryer, don't you, love?' she leans in close to Nancy's ear, and Nancy nods in agreeance.

Candy carefully places the dryer over Nancy's head and turns it on, before joining me in the room at the back of the salon where I've got the kettle boiling and have cleared space amongst the colour pots, rollers and other hairdressing paraphernalia.

Candy groans with pleasure as she puts a warm muffin into her mouth, her cute dimples appearing.

'Better than sex with a sexy cowboy,' she says, winking at me.

I blush. 'No more cowboys for me. I've moved on, one hundred percent. Cowboys don't even cross my mind for a minute anymore,' I lie, the memory of Quinton still creeping into my thoughts, most strongly as I lay in bed trying to fall asleep with Jackson beside me, wishing he was Quinton.

I try to shift Candy off the topic of Quinton, knowing she wants to dine out on my cowboy crush every time we are together.

'I should hope not, now that you've got your rich, ambitious Jackson at your disposal,' Candy says. 'I hear he's moving back to town permanently.'

I look up sharply. 'Where did you hear that?'

'I have my ways. I do work in a hairdressing salon, after all.'

'I know that, but how can news travel that fast? He only just mentioned it to me as an idea less than an hour and a half ago.'

Candy laughs. 'He dropped in to make a hair appointment on his way to some big meeting.'

'I see, yes, he's heading off late tomorrow.'

'Yeah, I couldn't fit him in, so I said I'd drop round early in the morning and give him a haircut at home.'

'Personalised service!'

'It's really just an excuse to check out your amazing house.'

'It's not my house, it's Jackson's house. I'm just house sitting.'

'That's what you call it? House sitting? I'd call it house sitting with fringe benefits.'

I blush. 'No, just house sitting.'

'Liar. I can see it all over your face. You're having non-stop sex with him. You've fallen back into your ex-boyfriend's arms, broken-hearted from your cowboy love and now Jackson is *your* rebound.'

'He is not my rebound and I am simply house sitting,' I say adamantly with a serious face, before I crumple. 'I guess if there's a little bit of sex on the side, there's nothing really wrong with that, is there?'

Candy roars with laughter. 'No, there is absolutely nothing wrong with that! I knew it. I knew you were having sex! You look a whole lot better than you've looked in ages, and that's what I was putting it down to.'

'Stop! It's not the sex. It's the contentment of my new life and my new jobs at the nursery and the club. I have a much better balance.'

I never went back to the piggery after that heartbreakingly awkward conversation with Quinton about Beth coming home. I dropped into the RSL Club that night on my way home and started a new job the next day. The following weekend while I was in the nursery chatting up a storm about plants with the owner Mrs Mac, she asked if I could come in and help out a couple of days a week. She's been there as long as I can remember, and having me around means she can go home early every now and then and put her tired feet up.

'I'm calling it, if this big meeting ends up landing Jackson back in town, he's going to pop the question and you're it,' Candy says with a flourish.

'That's the most ridiculous thing I've heard come out of your mouth, and there's been plenty,' I protest.

'Don't be so modest,' Candy says. 'He's in love with you. He always has been obsessed and now I think he wants to come back, settle down, get married and have a tribe of kids. Who better to fulfil his dreams than the beautiful Skye?'

'Stop it, Candy. Now you are talking absolute shit,' I laugh as I check my watch and get up to leave.

'Gotta go, I'll leave you here with your plate of muffins and to spread vicious rumors that aren't true about me and Jackson for the rest of your day.'

'Very well then. You have a good day pottering about with all your plants. Could not think of anything more boring than working at a plant shop.'

She rolls her eyes, and I roll mine in return.

'And I couldn't think of anything more boring than standing around playing with people's hair all day.'

I leave by the back door, still needing to clear my head. Is Candy right? Is Jackson in love with me, and is he arranging something more permanent under the guise of asking me to be his house sitter?

I know I have to move on from Quinton. He is a dream that is never going to come true. The question I ask myself daily is why am I obsessing over him? The way he asked me to leave my job, the job I worked in long before he arrived, the job I have loved since I was sixteen years old, to make things easier on himself, is inexcusable.

Anger is the only emotion that will allow me to move on. I muster more of it. Who is he to walk into my life, lead me on then take everything away from me? Yes, I am angry with him. Maybe I even hate him.

My strides get faster and I pump my arms as I mumble under my breath.

'That's right, Quinton. You can go and get stuffed. Why am I even giving you a moment of my thought time?'

I put my shoulders back and walk resolutely to the garden centre, four blocks away. I pass the heady, sweet smell of a flowering honeysuckle and breathe in its beauty.

It takes my mind off Quinton and with the fresh air filling my lungs my surroundings come into clearer focus. The familiar gardens between Candy's salon and my new nursery workplace with colourful roses lining concrete pathways, white picket fences with generous pale pink hydrangea drooping lazily while busy bees buzz

in and out of their centres. Purple wisteria growing over gate arch-
ways and ornamental grape vines winding up and along to provide
dense shade on timber pergolas.

I love this town so much. I love my new job at the nursery and am
finding it a real luxury to be around plants all day. My main job at the
club is okay, I could take it or leave it, but it's better than sitting
around at home at night feeling sorry for myself. The busier I stay the
better, that way I can fall into an exhausted sleep at night.

I am loving my independence and freedom living in Jackson's
beautiful house. What if that one day becomes our house, our home?

I picture myself in it, living happily ever after with my big, ambitious, energetic man.

*Interesting thought: Sometimes settling for second best can turn out to
be the best.*

14

CANDY

I am climbing the walls. As much as I love Skye to the end of the earth, a tiny sliver of jealousy turned up uninvited a couple of weeks ago that my best friend has it all and I don't.

She has the rich, good-looking landlord, who doubles as her fuck buddy whenever he comes home. As messy as it was, she also had the sexiest cowboy in town fawning over her.

'Not fair,' I mutter to myself as I hang out the washing. 'Here I am, barely able to make ends meet with my low paying job at the hair-dressing salon and Skye has it all, two sexy men at her beck and call, and both are loaded.'

Having both been brought up by single mums and neither of us having much money, we made our own clothes and our own fun. We were inseparable all through primary and high school, so much so that people wouldn't refer to us by our individual names – we were *Skandy*. When Jackson came along and started to show interest in Skye, I was maddeningly jealous. Not because she had a boyfriend and I didn't, but because I didn't want to share *my* Skye with anyone.

Yet she always included me, and we became a happy trio. Then there was that one night, many moons ago, when our trio became a threesome. This was the night I fell in love with Jackson. The way he kissed and took command of me. Not to mention the way he fucked me. However, he didn't choose me. I was just there to help him live out his fantasy, a fantasy where I was needed only to play a part, then exit stage left.

I wished Skye and I could go back to the way we were before that night. It was a simpler time where our love and deep friendship for each other was the most important thing in the world to us both. Skye and I never spoke of that night again, and through her silence she's made it clear she never wants to.

I have always dreamed of living happily ever after with the love of my life in a country house with a white picket fence and a tribe of kids in tow – a house just like the one Skye is living in. It is Jackson's face that comes to mind in my picket fence dream. It should be me living in that house, not her.

I want to be the girlfriend, then the wife of someone who will provide for me, treasure me and lavish me with love and security. Jackson. I want a practical man, someone who can fix things, make things. Jackson. My clock started ticking extra loudly when I turned twenty-one last year. I truly thought I would be married by now, *bare foot and pregnant*. Some of our school friends are having their second child, but whenever I try to land my perfect husband, he never seems to stick.

Everybody around town knows if they want a good time, they'll get one with me. Problem is, nobody wants to settle down with the good time girl.

It's my day off but I promised Jackson I'd cut his hair. It is really just an excuse to check out the house. I am dressed in cut-off denim shorts and in the mirror I turn my head to admire my generous bum cheeks peeking suggestively out the bottom. The strap of my lacy hot pink bra is just visible underneath the thin straps of my white low-cut singlet that shows off my full, voluptuous breasts which are whiter than a nun's tit. If anyone decides to look more closely, and I know they will, they'll get the hint of a small tattoo of a red rose on my left bosom.

I take the front steps two at a time.

'Woohooo!' I call out as I knock loudly. While I'm waiting I admire the cottage garden which is in full bloom with flowers of all colours, shapes and sizes. I groan inwardly. Skye and her plants. She would spend her whole life in a garden if she could. I hate gardening. Although I must admit Skye has things around here looking pretty.

The door opens to reveal a bare-chested, sweating, six-pack Jackson in loose, mid-thigh length gym shorts. His curly, dark-brown hair has formed ringlets which my hairdressing scissors are begging to tame.

'Hey, Jackson, I'm a bit early for your haircut, but thought I'd take the opportunity to have a squiz at your new place,' I say in a rush, as the blood rushes to my hair roots at the sight of him.

'All good,' Jackson says to my chest, his eyes landing, as I anticipated, on the delicate red petals of my rose tattoo. 'I was just finishing up. Make yourself at home.'

I follow him into the kitchen, admiring the classy white wainscoting up the full length of the wide hallway. A crystal chandelier hangs about halfway along, raising the decadence of this country home renovation.

'Wow, the doctor's wife didn't hold back on the décor,' I gush.

'No, she didn't. There's a photo album of before and after in the study, along with photos of when it was originally built. Skye's been down at the historical society looking for more garden photos, she wants to get it looking like it used to.'

I swallow my envy. Of course she does.

Jackson reaches into the fridge and pulls out two bottles of water, throwing one at me.

'Think quick,' he winks.

'Fancy, just like in the shops,' I fumble slightly but thankfully don't drop it on the timber topped island bench which is straight from the pages of *Country Style* magazine.

'All they drink out there is bottled water. When I come home, I just can't get used to the town water around here, disgusting.'

'Sure is. I don't know how they expect people to drink that shit.'

'I'm getting some new tanks installed soon, then we won't need the town water at all.'

I try not to stare at Jackson's bare chest, long waist, or the thin line of hair that disappears down the front into his low-slung gym shorts.

'Thanks for coming round on your day off for the haircut,' Jackson says as he runs his hands through his unruly hair. 'It needs taming.'

His words send a jolt to my core. I'd love to be tamed.

'Not a problem at all.'

I look around the open plan kitchen-dining area.

'This is real nice Jackson. You must be making the big bucks to be able to afford this before you're twenty-five.'

'Twenty-eight,' he replies. 'I'm getting old.'

'Not very. You don't look it.' I flush as we make strong eye contact, him on one side of the island bench, me on the other.

'Pretty tidy too for a bachelor's pad.'

'Thanks to Skye. Picking up after me. She's a good house sitter.'

I roll my eyes. 'She always has been anal about keeping things straight. Uugghh, drives me mad the way she follows me around picking up my mess.'

'Not me,' Jackson grins. 'Best thing I ever did was ask her to house sit.'

'Of course you'd say that. What man doesn't want someone picking up after him?'

I finish my water and hand the bottle back.

'I know you've got stuff to do, so I'll get to it. I've left my scissor kit in the car. Maybe set a chair up in the bathroom,' I say as I skip up the hallway. 'Easier to clean up and you don't want to find bits of hair in your food if I do it out here.'

My heart is racing by the time I get back inside. I'm so unfit. Not like Skye, who runs ten kilometres without raising a sweat.

He's obediently sitting in front of a large oval mirror centred between two intricate, stained-glass windows. I put my kit down on the long bench which runs the full length of the wall. A large sink with gold taps sits in a timber vanity underneath the mirror. Black and white retro checkerboard tiles are cool on my bare feet.

I peg an old sheet that I found in the laundry around his broad shoulders and go into work mode.

'To stop the hair from sticking on you,' I say. 'Nice bathroom by the way.'

'Yes, fanciest bathroom I've ever washed in. There's an ensuite too, it's got the same tiles and everything but just on a smaller scale.'

'I never took you for being so into house décor Jackson. I always thought you were more of a blokey bloke.'

'Don't tell anyone.' He winks at me as I comb his hair into place ready to cut.

'Your secret's safe with me.'

I flush from the way he's staring.

'What about the garden, is that another one of your secret passions?' I ask, snipping at his curls expertly.

'Nah, that's all Skye. She's always in the garden, hardly see her.'

'Same, she's busy busy, that's for sure. Between her two jobs at the nursery and the club, growing veggies with her Mum and trying to get a bit of a thing going at the markets, the time she spends at the soup kitchen and living here which is much further from my house than Bev's, I feel like I never see her these days.'

Jackson doesn't reply. I look up to see him eyeing off my erect nipples poking through my skimpy singlet.

He sees me catch his stare. 'Cold, are you?'

'Yes, it is cool in here,' I say softly.

Jackson smiles suggestively as I continue to snip.

'As I was saying, you've set up things pretty well for yourself. Installing your very own gardener and housekeeper to look after things while you're away.'

'True that,' he agrees. 'We've got ourselves a pretty good arrangement.'

'What sort of arrangement exactly? Is it serious between you two?' I ask casually as I run my fingers through his hair to check if my cuts are even.

'Dunno, could be,' Jackson says. 'Skye is holding back though. You know what she's like. Doesn't seem to want to settle down.'

I keep quiet, waiting for him to elaborate.

'When we first started going out, she was young. We have fun when I come home but she's very arm's length.'

'Maybe it's because you broke her heart.'

'I did?'

'Yes, you did. She pined after you for months. I could hardly get her out of bed some days.'

'I had no idea. I thought that's what she wanted.'

'Of course you thought that. Men are so thick, you know. You have no idea how to treat a woman.'

'Hey, that's a bit rough,' Jackson protests.

'Truth hurts,' I tease. 'She's not going to fall for that again, especially when you're so far away.'

'That won't be forever. As soon as I've got enough money together, I'm planning to come back here and set up my own business.'

'Oh, yeah, like what?'

'Earthmoving. We get all the training in the mines to drive these huge, massive machines. It gets pretty lonely out there and I miss being here around family and friends, so I've been trying to work out a way to get myself set up to come home.

'I bought that block out in the new industrial area and have this idea to buy my own fleet of machines then start putting some of those skills into practice. There'll be plenty of work. That's what my big meeting was about.'

'That sounds fantastic,' I say. 'I'm impressed.'

'Best thing I did was get out of this small town, go and see the world a bit. You and Skye should probably do the same one day.'

'I'm not interested in seeing the world. I'm happy right here. I love this town. I never want to be anywhere else. And you'll never get Skye to leave. Her feet are concreted into the pavement. Just like her Mum.'

I move around to cut his fringe. 'Close your eyes, so you don't get hair in them.'

'Yes Ma'am,' he says obediently, closing his eyes. 'You smell good.'

'You don't,' I laugh.

'Haha, well, I've been working out, you know.'

'Yes, you have,' I say suggestively as I carefully cut around his forehead.

He moves his hands out from underneath the sheet to grab me by the hips.

'Whoa, careful, or you'll lose an eye.'

I stop cutting, and he opens his eyes, coming face to face with my breasts.

'Sorry, not sorry,' he says as he continues to hold onto my hips while I cut. I reach behind me without moving to get the soft hair brush.

He slowly moves his fingers around the top of my shorts, touching my silky smooth skin while I brush the hair from his face. As I lean around to brush the back of his neck and unclip the peg, I feel his hot breath between my breasts. He lets go of my hips as I deftly remove the sheet, scoop up the hair around the chair and push it into the corner.

Feeling self-conscious now that I'm done, I turn around to wash my hands. Jackson reaches up underneath my shorts to cup my soft cheeks. I try and turn around, but he forces me to stay where I am so he can watch my face in the mirror as he moves his fingers up inside my shorts and rubs them along the lace of my matching hot pink G-string. He pulls the string out from between my cheeks and continues to watch my face as he deftly slips two fingers into me.

'You're wet,' he says.

'What do you expect? Have you looked at yourself lately, Jackson? You're a hunk of spunk.'

He leans down to kiss me on the side of the neck. We don't break eye contact in the mirror. I pant quietly as he moves his fingers inside me, plunging deeper and faster.

With one quick movement he pulls down my shorts, tosses aside my G-string and goes down on his knees, moving my legs apart so he can plunge his tongue inside me.

I climax instantly; my moans and soft, gentle whimpers echoing around the bathroom.

He stands, turns me to face him and moves my hand down to his hard cock which is straining against his gym shorts.

'It looks like you need a bit of attention,' I say, as I pull his shorts down and kneel. He grabs at my shoulder-length blonde curls and pushes my face into him until his huge cock is stuffed inside my mouth. I gag as he thrusts into me. I can hardly fit him in. He gets harder and harder, faster and faster, then lets go; filling my mouth with his salty, warm, sticky liquid. I swallow as I stand, wiping escaping drops from the side of my mouth.

'That's not usually part of the service,' I say.

'It should be,' he winks and pulls me into the shower. I'm still wearing my singlet and bra but he doesn't notice. 'I think a hair wash should also be part of the service'. He hands me the shampoo and I squeeze it into my hands and through his hair.

'This definitely should be part of the service,' he says, his eyes closed while I massage his scalp. When I'm done shampooing I get the conditioner, leaning into his back while my fingers slip through his hair. I move him under the shower to rinse.

'There, all done,' I say.

'Not quite,' Jackson says, opening the shower door to retrieve the chair.

'Kneel,' he commands, 'and spread those luscious arse cheeks for me.'

I obey. He starts soaping my ripe cheeks and I spread wider for him so he can see everything.

He gently eases a finger inside me, then another, while using his other hand to run along his shaft. I reach behind and feel it, soft at first then gradually getting harder.

'You have the biggest cock I've ever had,' I say, helping him tug and pull and bring it back to life. It works and I encircle it with my hand while he guides his fingers in and out of me.

'You love it from behind, don't you, Candy,' he growls.

'I do. I especially love your big cock from behind. Give it to me,' I beg. He is in no mood to wait and I gasp as he plunges hard into me, a sharp pain followed by ecstasy.

'You're tight,' he says, as he fucks me harder. The combination of the shower steam, the soap, the pain and the thrill of what he is doing, makes me want to faint and scream at the same time.

He is done in less than ten seconds, and I can feel his cum dribbling out as he pulls away. He has taken me all for himself, leaving me hanging. He washes and steps out of the shower without another word.

I am still wearing my singlet and bra. I wash, wincing in pain after how rough he was. I dry myself off and find a T-shirt of his in the washing basket. I gather my things, including my wet clothes.

Jackson is eating a sandwich when I walk into the kitchen.

'Well,' I say with false brightness, 'anytime you need a haircut, just give me call.'

He nods towards a $50 note on the bench. 'Payment,' he says, and manages to make me feel like dirt on the bottom of his shoe. 'Also, Skye is never to know.'

With as much dignity as I can muster, I take the money and let myself out the door.

15

SKYE

The beer fridge is packed, the bar is wiped down and I'm ready for the next onslaught which is only minutes away. The roar of the crowd in the dying minutes of the game drifts through the doors and I wonder if Scone Thoroughbreds can pull off another grand final win this year. They've notched up a few in the past decade, dominating the league for most of the 1990s.

It's my first night working the bar for the football club, but after working my way up in the RSL Club from waitress to bar person to bar manager, I'm in familiar territory.

I haven't had time to watch the game, keeping the cold beers up to the crowd who have come from far and wide to see if their dream team can make it three in a row. Word around the street is all about their new recruit, a cowboy who rode in on a shiny horse and is going to keep the club on its winning streak.

My dream cowboy. *My* want, *my* need, *my* can't have.

I haven't seen or heard much of either Quinton or Beth since that devastating day when I walked away from the farm I loved. Austin drops around regularly like he always has, but he steers well clear of any conversations about them. I don't know if Quinton has confided in him, or if he just knows something was going on between us, but I'm not about to say anything.

I go along with the bar banter about the cowboy recruit, convinced I have moved on thanks to the anger I've nurtured. I tell myself daily that I am still annoyed, mad in fact, for how Quinton turned my world upside down when he sacked me.

I've been nervously looking out for Beth all day, worrying how I'll be able to look her in the eye, especially if Quinton ended up telling her the truth.

I shake my head in annoyance. Why am I even letting these thoughts in? I am fully content with my new life with Jackson, who will be home full-time soon. *Time heals all wounds* is an old saying, and it's true. Partly.

The final siren goes and I can't help myself. I race out the doors to watch the crowd surge onto the field and lift the hero of the game onto their shoulders.

Car horns honk, people cheer, whistle and yahoo and I zoom in on a grinning Quinton, with his wild wavy hair and muscly arms glistening with training oil and sweat. Try as I might to sustain my anger, I am transfixed and get caught up in the atmosphere. As Quinton gets closer I cheer along with everyone else; clapping, yelling and roaring excitedly. They let him down just a few metres from me. People are shaking their cans and spraying beer all over him. Someone hands him a freshly-opened can, and he takes a long, thirsty swig.

As he turns around, his full masculinity on show, he spots me in the crowd.

'Hey, Skye,' he says, lifting me effortlessly and landing a kiss right on my lips, before putting me down and continuing with his team mates to the clubrooms.

Stunned, I look around wildly, worried Beth will see what has just happened. What did just happen?

Puzzled, I return to the bar and have no time to think about it.

It's much later when I see Quinton again. Showered, dressed in denim jeans, a chambray blue button-down shirt tucked into his neat waist, showing off a large belt buckle I haven't seen before. He saunters towards the bar in his cowboy boots and trademark Akubra.

'How's it going?' he asks shyly.

'I'm fine. Actually, I'm more than fine,' I reply icily.

'That's good to hear, I have thought of you often,' he says. I look sharply at him.

'You have? Why? I would have thought you'd have wiped all memory of me from your mind.'

Quinton lowers his eyes, and my heart does a little flutter when I see him blush. My anger dissipates and I admonish myself. Bev has taught me not to hold grudges. *It does you no good, love.*

'I'm going pretty good,' I say, changing tone, although I still have a nervous quiver. 'More to the point, how are you going? Bit of a hero around here from all the bar talk.'

'Yeah, good. It's been a good day,' he says humbly. 'I don't know about being a hero. I didn't really do much, just part of the team.'

'They're talking you up big time.'

He leans in close and lowers his voice. 'It's a bit embarrassing actually, I'm not that good. I never was all that good. I'm not a superstar or a natural or anything. But it's such a good team. Never seen anything like it.'

'You're just an all-round nice guy, aren't you, Quinton,' I say, my voice laced with sarcasm as I pass him a beer. 'This one's on the house. Cheers to the club's new recruit.'

'Cheers,' Quinton winks as he opens the can and takes a sip, leaving me in a state of complete disrepair.

'I'll have to do a bit more training for next season, it's knocked me around. Didn't realise how unfit I was.'

'I told you if you played footy you'd have to put in some more time. The usual farm work just doesn't cut it.'

'I know, you were right, I was wrong,' he admits. I try to regain composure while my stomach flips over itself again, then realise he's still talking. 'Might take you up on helping me set a training regime. Teach me how to train properly so I don't spend three days recovering after every game.'

I pick up empty glasses from along the bar and put them in the dishwasher.

'How's your training going?' he asks.

'Oh, you're still here.'

'Yeah, still here. I need a rest but don't tell anyone.'

My smile spreads a familiar warmth over me.

'I won't. My training is good. I'm preparing for the Coolangatta Gold.'

'Coolangatta, the one Grant Kenny did in that movie?'

'Yep, that's the one.'

'Impressive.'

Quinton leans casually against the bar, oblivious to the way he has my heart racing. I can't believe I haven't seen him since that conversation under the maple tree. It's taken serious effort and dedication to erase him from my mind. Who am I kidding though? I'll never be able to erase him.

'It's just a marathon. A challenging one, but not impossible.'

I look around to see if anyone else needs serving, but for the first time all day it seems there's nobody at the bar, just Quinton and I.

'How's life?' he asks.

'All good. I've moved into a new place, house sitting for...a mate.'

'In town?'

'Yes, the old doctor's house. It's nice. Has a huge garden. It wasn't really planned, it just sort of happened. A good mate of mine who I've known since high school bought it. He works away, in the mines, and needed someone to look after it, and I'm that someone.'

Quinton raises his eyebrow.

'No, no, it's nothing like that,' I assure him, wondering why I can't tell him Jackson is my boyfriend. At that moment the crowd returns, saving me from any further questioning.

'Anyway, nice to see you Quinton, have a good night. I'll catch you later.'

'No worries, nice to see you too.'

The crowd swallows him, and I am left with a jumble of emotions and a tingling fanny that is screaming out for my true love cowboy's touch.

...

IT'S WELL AFTER MIDNIGHT, down to the final few stragglers, and I closed the bar.

'Off you go, time to go home. Make sure you have a safe driver,' I yell as they wobble out the door towards their cars. 'Yes, Mum,' they yell back.

'And if you don't have a safe driver, I'll call you a cab.'

'Yes Mum,' a few call back. I shake my head, knowing that someone who shouldn't will get behind the wheel. I just hope everyone gets home safely, especially Quinton. From the number of beers I've seen him consume, he will be in no state to drive.

All of a sudden it feels urgent I find him. I race outside, coming across a group huddled around a fire in an old kerosene drum. Sure enough, Quinton is there, wearing his wobbly boots. I wander over, casually addressing the whole crowd.

'You boys planning to stay here tonight? Or is anyone going to be stupid enough and get in and drive themselves home?'

'We'll probably stay,' Billy says. Billy, a local farmer, is team captain, and stands ten foot taller as captain of a premiership team.

'Righto, if you're staying, hand those keys over,' I say in my bossiest voice. Billy reaches into his pockets and hands me his keys. I go from player to player. Eventually I get to Quinton.

'Hand them over, Quinton.'

'Nah, I'll be right. I won't drive,' he says, swaying as he speaks.

'That's what they all say. Best bet is to give your keys to me. I'll keep them safe until you're sober enough to get behind the wheel.'

'I'm going on the waters, and when I've sobered up, I'll drive home,' Quinton says petulantly. 'I've driven home in a worst state than this.'

'You're not in the outback anymore, cowboy. The roads are a lot windier around here than out where you come from. Hand me your keys.'

Quinton refuses. Frustrated, I put my hands into his pockets. He puts one arm around me and pulls me in tight.

'Or you could drive me home,' he says, his voice husky. There's a roar from the rest of the boys.

'Or I could just take your keys, and you can stay here and party on with the lads,' I say, ignoring the way he is making my legs feel like they're made of butter. I pull his keys out of his pocket and reluctantly step away. Satisfied I have all keys I raise my voice.

'You might not all remember in the morning, but to get your keys back, find your way to old Doctor Booth's house after three. If I think you're sober enough to drive, you'll get your keys back. Good night. Have fun.'

'Don't go, Skye,' they protest. 'Stay and party with us.'

'I've got work tomorrow. Plus, I'm buggered from working my guts out behind the bar, making sure the beers stay cold and making sure you've all had fun.'

As I climb into bed, I'm still puzzling over Quinton and Beth but try and force myself to think about Jackson. I am living in this beautiful house. I don't need to complicate things by fantasising about Quinton removing his cowboy boots, belt and hat and climbing in beside me, stripping me naked and finishing what we never got to finish.

I go over our conversation at the bar. My conversations with Jackson versus my conversations with Quinton are polar opposites. Jackson is easygoing, a big talker but not a big listener. In a group, he holds court with story after story, each getting more elaborate the more times he tells them. When it's the two of us, he's more interested in my body than my brains. He has never asked me about my own goals, my own dreams. It's not that he's unkind, it's just that he believes the whole world centres around him.

I shouldn't complain. He gives me everything else I ever wanted. I don't want to leave Scone; this is my hometown and I have no ambition to live anywhere else. I am living in a beautiful home. While Jackson is away, my time is my own for my own hobbies, my own work, to hang out with Candy, to go round to Mum's. What more could a girl want? As I drift into an exhausted sleep a final thought pitter patters through my head.

Quinton, that's what more a girl wants.

...

I PULL into the garage after a busy day at the nursery – the job I really love. The RSL is busy and challenging but it's my days with Mrs Mac in the nursery, which doubles as a flower shop, that I love the most.

Sundays are always busy, especially when it is warm and sunny. When I go for a run later, I know I'll spot a lot of new garden plants around town. I brought home a tray of plants for Jackson's garden, which I've transformed from the bedraggled and neglected state it was in after the house was empty for a few months waiting to be sold. It has been a labour of love to bring this beautiful garden back to life.

There is no vegetable garden, though, and I'll have to speak to Jackson about rectifying that. I've got a few ideas of where it should go but I will need to build a structure first and maybe a dedicated gardening shed.

As I walk around the front to sit my plant tray on the verandah, I scream, startled to see Quinton on the top step, his cowboy hat beside him.

'Hey! You gave me a fright.'

'What's all the screaming about?' he groans, putting his hands over his ears.

'Very funny. How long have you been here?'

'An hour or so.'

'You're looking a bit worse for wear.'

'I'm all right. Could be better.'

'I'm surprised to see you already. Usually the boys don't show up for their keys for a week or so.'

'A week?'

'Yeah, it's a tradition, and all the wives and girlfriends just have to suck it up as their husbands and boyfriends go from pub to pub, house to house, drinking constantly day and night to celebrate the big win.'

'Never heard of that before.'

'Probably because where you come from, it's too far from pub to pub and house to house.'

'True. But a whole week? What about work, chores, responsibilities?'

'They all go out the window. Footy players' privilege.'

'I couldn't do it. I've got too much to do and one big night of drinking is enough for me.'

'You mean a night and a day?' I laugh. 'Have you been to bed yet?'

'No, not yet.'

'Is Beth looking after the pigs?'

'No, Austin's got that under control and gave me the day off. Beth has gone back to Sydney.'

I am afraid to ask if gone means gone, or just gone back to work, and my stomach twists into knots. I sit down next to him, putting the plants down.

'This is my boyfriend's house,' I say quietly.

Quinton's shoulders stiffen. 'Boyfriend? I didn't know you had a boyfriend.'

'I've had this boyfriend, of sorts, since I was in high school. His name's Jackson.'

'Jackson. I see. So you've always had a boyfriend, since we first met?'

I jump in quickly. 'No, no. Not always. Not then. Not for ages when you first bought the farm. We used to be pretty serious for a couple of years, then he moved away for work. We'd catch up sometimes when he came home, but we hadn't been boyfriend and girl-friend for a long time when you and I met.'

Quinton stares at me intently and I'm conscious of waffling.

'After I left the piggery, we started spending a bit of time together when he was home on leave. One thing led to another, and what do you know, I'm living in his house.'

Quinton looks away. 'I see. It's none of my business, sorry. That's good.'

'Yeah, it is good,' I reply, my voice wavering.

What would be good is for Quinton to look at me intently again, and to never stop.

He doesn't.

'Anyway, I'll go and get your keys.'

'Thanks, Skye.'

When I get back Quinton is laying sideways on the verandah, obviously in no state to drive. I shake his shoulder gently. 'How about I drive you home and you come and get your ute later in the week, grab a lift with Austin or something.'

He sits up quickly, running his hands through his glorious thick hair. He attempts to stand and falls straight back down.

'Um, yeah. Maybe, if you sure?'

I'm laughing. 'Yes, I'm sure. You absolutely cannot drive.'

'What about your plants? It looks like you had the whole after-noon worked out.'

'They can wait. It's not going to take me long to get you home.'

As I drive along the familiar road I used to take every day, nostalgia drifts in and out of my open window. I turn into the gate which leads to the homestead, and look in admiration at the freshly-mown lawns and neat garden.

'You've got the garden looking schmick. I sure do miss it out here,' I say.

'Why don't you come back?'

'I can't. I've got two jobs I love, working at the RSL and the nursery.'

'Quit them, just come back. It's not the same without you, we can't find anyone as good as you.'

'And you never will,' I joke, trying to deflect.

Quinton puts his strong, calloused hand on my arm and his warmth burns my skin.

'I'm really sorry, Skye, for what happened. You know that, don't you?'

'It's fine,' I say briefly, wanting to pull my arm away but not hating his hand on me. 'We've all moved on. Life works out is exactly as it should.'

I feel a chill as he moves his hand away.

'I guess.' His voice is flat. 'The offer's there, if you ever change your mind.'

'Thanks, but I'm pretty tied up, you know, with Jackson's house and everything.'

'That's right, of course.'

We sit in an awkward silence. 'Anyway, the best thing for you, I reckon, is a hot shower and a big sleep, Quinton.'

Reluctantly he opens his door. 'You're right. Sleep will be good.'

I drive away quickly, not trusting myself to be in his company for too much longer. He probably won't remember anything either of us have said since I found him on Jackson's front verandah.

As I drive home, I wind down the window and shake Quinton off my shoulder. I'm not going to fall back into his strong arms, not now, not ever. I've moved on. When he said Beth was gone, he probably just meant she was back at work which means she will be here again soon.

My anger creeps in. He has no right to come crawling back and offering me my old job, after he was the one who told me to leave.

Selling my sacking as not wanting me to feel uncomfortable around Beth when she got out of hospital, even though it was him who didn't want to feel uncomfortable or be reminded of what he'd done.

I've moved on. Jackson is my man and I am living the dream. I'm not going to let a hot, football-playing cowboy with piercing blue eyes and arse-hugging Wrangler jeans take me off course.

16

JACKSON

J ust because I had sex with Candy, it doesn't mean I was being
unfaithful. Right?

Skye has long made it clear she and I are just casual,
nothing serious, just a brief fling when I'm home.

Having sex with Candy surely doesn't count as cheating when
Skye isn't fully committed. Right? For all I know, I could be one of
many suitors.

As the months pass, I know in my heart Skye is falling for me
again and I have a niggling thought which won't go away. The physical torture of working in these conditions in a constant ball of sweat
and exhaustion is creating a mental torture of desperately wanting to
be with her.

I want to go back to how we used to be, before I moved away. We
were the perfect pair. Side by side, with our matching dark hair and
strikingly similar long and lean physiques, we look great together.

Until Candy told me, I didn't realise I'd broken Skye's heart. I
thought I was doing the right thing. I am much older, and by the time
we started going out I'd lived a full life, had been with a lot of women
and travelled the world. She was still in high school and had hardly

left Scone's town limits. I thought if we broke up, she might branch out and see some of the world for herself.

She never did. I understand now. She's content here. It's where she sees her past, present and future. I could make that future brighter.

She would be the perfect wife. She is kind, gorgeous, a great cook, a beautiful homemaker, and keeps the garden immaculate. I want a tribe of children, boys, mostly, but then a girl for Skye. I adore everything about her. She is pliable and easygoing.

What more could a man want?

Candy. That's what. A pocket rocket full of energy and passion – physically the opposite to Skye's petite, fit frame with her curves and plenty to hold onto. She is hot, and sex with her is blindingly wild. She is a good time girl.

For as long as I can remember, they have come as a pair and never venture far from each other. I toy with the fantasy of a re-run of that night when they were eighteen. I've gotten myself off on the memory many a time out here in the lonely desert after a long, hard day.

I'm dreaming though. Skye has made it clear it was a one-off.

My heart sinks at the memory of her tears as she watched me fucking Candy, something I should never have done that night. Candy, something I also should never have done when she came around for that haircut.

She is more than a handful and definitely not marriage material, she'd be far too much maintenance.

Candy will never happen again, I promise myself.

I want to change the status of my relationship with Skye from casual to committed. It is Skye I want to live happily ever after with. I want to get home so my life with Skye can work out exactly how it's meant to be.

...

As I SIT at the island bench watching her potter about my kitchen, making breakfast, it hits me like a lightning flash. I want Skye for the rest of my days, in my kitchen, in my garden, in my bed. Permanently in every part of my life.

As though she can read my thoughts, she turns around and smiles, lighting me up from the inside out.

'What?' she asks.

'Nothing. Just admiring how sexy you look in my kitchen.'

Skye comes around to where I'm sitting and wraps herself around me like a sleek, purring cat.

'It's a pretty nice kitchen.'

'It suits you,' I murmur as I kiss her suggestively on the nape of the neck. 'And you suit me.'

The sound of the toaster popping up breaks our spell and Skye returns to breakfast preparations.

'It's a pretty nice house. I feel lucky to be living here – in my wildest dreams I never imagined living in a house like this.'

She hands me my toast, buttered and spread with vegemite just the way I like it.

'As I've been saying, I'm not going to be away much longer. This is my very last stint and then I'm back, for good. I've saved up enough and I'm going to start my earthmoving business as soon as I'm done with the mines.'

'Congratulations!' Skye's delight is genuine.

'I'm so proud of you Jackson,' she continues. 'You're going to get so much work, there's no stopping you.'

She comes around to sit beside me and share my vegemite toast. I admire her perfect posture and long bare legs extending from the stool.

'You know, I'm happy to move back home so you can have the place all to yourself. Bev keeps telling me she is lonely without me!'

I reach out and grab her hand, pulling it into me.

'I know you think I just asked you to live here so I had a house sitter to keep things nice. But you should know, Skye, you mean a lot more to me than that.' I hope she can't see the guilt behind my eyes and I silently promise her, and myself, that I'll never stray again.

She smiles her beautiful, wide, trusting smile.

'I'm not asking for any promises from you Jackson. We've been down that road before, and it didn't work. And as much as I think you're great and amazing, I don't expect anything from you.'

I put my finger to her lips.

'Skye, beautiful Skye. How can you not know how much I love you?'

Skye's eyes widen and she flushes.

I stand and she wraps her legs around me. I lean down and kiss her, rubbing my hands all over her body. Effortlessly I lift her and carry her to the bedroom. The conversation is over for now, but I plan to continue it. I can see our lives clearly mapped out.

I toss her onto the bed and climb on top of her, pinning her arms so I can kiss her roughly on the lips. She breaks free and reaches her hands behind my head.

'Nice haircut, Candy told me you dropped into the salon,' she whispers as she runs her hands through my hair. I falter slightly. She doesn't notice and pulls me closer.

I spend the next hour convincing myself, and Skye, that we are the perfect match, and by the time we are fully spent and catching our breath, I have erased my slip-up with Candy completely from my mind, pretending she never happened.

17

SKYE

I am on the back veranda, feet up with a cold beer between my bare thighs, admiring the way the afternoon light glows up the garden.

'I'm planning to build a pool right here,' Jackson says, as he comes around the corner.

'Jackson!' I jump up to greet him. 'I didn't know you were coming home.'

'Surprise,' he says, scooping me up to kiss me and breathe in my familiar vanilla scent. 'I could get used to coming home to this every day,' he jokes as he puts me carefully down onto the chair, dragging another one close beside me.

'It's pretty nice this time of day. My favourite part,' I say, admiring the way his standard black T-shirt tucked into black jeans hugs his fit, lean body.

'You've got things looking good out here,' he says admiringly, taking a sip of my beer.

'Yeah, we've had some rain, makes all the difference. I've not long finished mowing and out of the shower. I was just thinking about cooking a barbecue chop for dinner, with a salad. I've got a kilo of chops so there's plenty for my hungry working man.'

Jackson grins at me, finishing off my beer.

'Got any more of these?' he asks.

'Always got plenty, but only Coronas. Can't stomach those green cans you seem to like so much.'

'A Corona will do. Hold the lemon.'

I laugh as I get two Coronas out, jamming the lemon into one and pushing it down before we clink bottles.

'Cheers to home sweet home. Am here for good this time.'

My heart flutters. It's the words I've been both dreading and dreaming to hear.

'So you really are done with the mines?'

'Yep, handed in my resignation, collected my big paycheck, jumped on a plane, picked up my car at the airport and had a night in Sydney. Such a great feeling to drive home knowing I'm here to stay. Was stinking hot this trip and I didn't want to be there.'

'I saw on the news, record temperatures, don't know how you do it. But you survived, and you're back to these beautiful mountains where it's lucky to reach thirty degrees on its hottest summer day.'

'I'll need to get myself a few more jumpers,' Jackson jokes.

The sun dips towards the horizon, and the last of the evening birds hum in the air.

'You should be proud Jackson, look at what you've achieved. You've worked hard, you've bought yourself a house, you've got a new car and you're about to start a new business. I'm impressed.'

'Thanks Skye, pretty good hey?'

I drain the last of my beer and get up to start the barbecue, expertly cooking the chops while Jackson looks on.

'I thought that was a man's job,' he says.

'Feel free to take over,' I laugh, 'but as far as I can see it, any man's job is also a woman's job.'

The smell of the sizzling chops fills the air.

'I've missed you, Skye.'

I raise my eyebrows, inquiringly. I'm still in two minds about what happens from here and have guarded my heart carefully in the lead-up to Jackson's permanent return. I haven't wanted to get too settled into this home and garden, but it's wrapped its arms around me and made me feel part of it.

'I reckon you're getting missing me mixed up with missing this beautiful house that I just happen to be looking after for you,' I say, continuing without a pause, 'I spoke to Mum; she's more than happy for me to move back. She gets a bit lonely with me not around.'

'I see.' Jackson stands and comes over to the barbecue and takes the tongs from me. 'I thought Bev would be loving the freedom and have her man move in. Mum and Dad couldn't wait for me to move out of home.'

'I'm sure she's had Bill over a time or two but she's a tough old bird. I don't think she'll be handing herself over fully to a man anytime soon. He's going to have to follow her rules, not the other way around.'

'What about you, Skye? Whose rules do you like to follow?' He hands the tongs back and stands behind me, nuzzling my neck as I turn the chops.

My stomach flips and I feel myself needing, wanting to be touched. I'd worked extra hard lately to rearrange my fantasies and desires, putting Quinton completely out of my mind, and focusing one hundred and ten percent on Jackson.

I could make this man happy. I could please him, nurture him, care for him.

'Smells good,' he says.

'Me or the chops,' I whisper.

'Both.'

A shiver runs down my back, and my knees are like jelly.

'They're nearly done,' I say, trying to focus. 'The salad is in the fridge.'

Jackson moves into the house, 'You want to eat out here?'

'Yeah, it's a nice night.'

'All we're missing is that pool. I'll get on to that tomorrow,' he says, as he brings out the salad, plates and sets the outdoor table.

'You should be saving your money for your business,' I say, not used to being around with someone with so much money.

'I've got plenty, and I've budgeted already for the pool. It will be great living out here in the summer, splashing around.'

We're eating, Jackson keeping the conversation flowing freely.

'For sure, I will definitely be coming over regularly for a sunbake and swim in your pool. You do know putting a pool in your backyard is how to make friends and influence people?'

I clear up after dinner while Jackson enjoys another beer on the verandah in the stillness of the night that has descended.

I am wiping down the island bench when he comes in, closing and locking the door behind him and pulling the blind.

'Getting a bit fresh out there,' he says, unzipping one of his bags that he'd brought in from the car. I don't see him slip something into his pocket.

'You must be tired,' I say, starting to feel awkward in my evening routine which is usually done solo. I gesture to his bags. 'Got any washing? I've got half a load, I could put it on now.'

'Yeah, a bit, but don't worry about that. I need a shower. And you.'

He pulls me close, kissing me fully on the lips. I melt into him and he lifts me easily. I wrap my legs around his waist and he carries me to the bathroom.

'Welcome home,' I whisper as I nibble on his earlobe from behind. He turns me around and pushes me against the shower wall, roughly, as is his way. His cock is hard and sticking straight out.

'Suck it,' he commands as he pushes me to my knees. I look up as I move my mouth over his cock, pulling it in. He grabs my long wet hair that's streaming down my back and pushes me into him, choking me as I suck and lick until I know he's about to burst.

He pulls me up to stand, cupping my small breasts in each hand and tweaking my nipples roughly. He devours them with his mouth and shoves his fingers inside me.

'Oh, you're wet,' he says as he licks and sucks on my nipples, his fingers pushing deeper and deeper.

He turns me around and commands me to pull my cheeks apart.

He lifts me slightly and shoves his cock straight into my wetness, holding both my hips as he shoves harder and harder. My forehead is against the wall, and I groan while he fucks me quickly.

'Skye Skye, you're so beautiful,' he says.

'Fuck me harder,' I scream.

He pulls out and turns me around, pulling me in close and kissing me roughly. He grabs my shoulders.

'I tell you how hard you get it,' he growls, as he shifts his hands down to pump his wet, slippery cock. 'Now, take it in the mouth and swallow it,' he orders, pushing me down to my knees again.

He lets go with a loud groan, holding my head into him so he can watch me swallow.

When he is done, he washes himself and steps out, leaving me under the shower in a ball of emotion. A tiny tear squeezes out of the corner of my eye. I try and convince myself that I love how Jackson takes charge and orders me around. How lucky I am to have such a strong, dominant man who knows exactly what he wants, and goes for it.

If that is the case, why do I feel so hollow?

18

SKYE

Jackson is gone when I wake up and I spend my time before work packing my things to move home.

I don't want him to think I am expecting anything more than the arrangement for me to housesit while he was away. Now that he's permanently back, we can go back to me listening out for the sound of his rumbling V8 coming around the corner and being casual fuck buddies.

When I get to the kitchen, I find a hurried note scribbled on the bench.

Sorry, had a super early meeting. See you tonight. Jackson x

Annoyance ruffles my hair from its roots. He's so sure of himself. Sure that I'll be waiting for him tonight. Sure that I'll still be here even though it's his house, not mine.

I park in the hairdresser's car park, as I do every day, and pop my head in to say hello to Candy and the girls.

'Skye Pie' Candy calls out as soon as she sees me. 'What muffins have you brought for me today?'

'Sorry Candy Mandy, no muffins today. I had to pack.'

'Pack for what?' Candy was giving a short, back and sides to Billy who came in from the farm for a monthly haircut.

'Hey, Skye,' he says shyly from underneath his black cape.

'Hey, Billy. How's it going?'

'Yeah, pretty good. You?'

'I'm good. What's happening out on the farm?'

'The usual, pretty dry at the moment, waiting for rain.'

'Shouldn't be too far away I wouldn't think. We got a shower in town the other day, mustn't have gotten out to you. Playing footy again this year?

'Yeah, we're gunna win again, make it four in a row.'

I laugh. 'You say that every year Billy. But I shouldn't make fun, because you're on a pretty good run.'

'Well, yeah, we're doin' alright. Four in a row will break league records, we're going to make it with our cowboy weapon. He's come back for another year and he's training pretty hard. He's going to take us right through.'

My stomach flips. 'Cowboy weapon?'

'You know Quinton, you used to work for him. When he turned up to training for a second year he got everyone pretty excited.'

I flush, of course I know exactly who Billy is talking about. Candy is watching me closely in the mirror but I refuse to return her gaze. The thought of running into Quinton at the footy again makes my heart race – the club has asked me to manage the bar every home game and the first one is next weekend, so there will be no way to avoid him.

Billy is oblivious to the spin he's sent me into.

'Still working at the plant shop and the RSL?' Billy asks.

'I'm sure Candy has kept you well up to date with all my news,' I say wryly, finally meeting her gaze with an eye roll.

'I sure have, I've been telling Billy how it's easier for you without having to travel out to the farm to work, plus you smell a whole lot better now you're not working with those stinky pigs.'

'I love those pigs,' I laugh. 'And they're not stinky, they're adorable.'

'Whatever Trevor, you were stinky, I'm telling you that for free.'

On that note, I say my goodbyes to Billy and head out the back to make Candy and I our morning cuppa. She hugs me from behind with a giggle. 'That sure did get your heart race up, hearing about your favourite cowboy on the footy team,' she teases.

'You're a bugger, Candy. You love seeing me squirm!'

'Sure do, I couldn't resist. From what I hear the whole team has a giant man crush on him.'

I don't trust myself to reply.

'Anyway, back to the fact you have no muffins for me because of packing. Where are you going?'

'Moving back home.'

I didn't notice Candy catch her breath. 'Home? Why?'

'Jackson is back, and for good this time. Our arrangement is done. I was only housesitting and looking after the garden while he was away.'

'Did you two have an argument?' Candy's voice is slightly high-pitched.

'No, nothing like that. I don't want him to think I'm expecting free rent and board now that there's not really any purpose for me being there.'

'None at all?' Candy winks.

'Haha, there is that. But I don't need to be living there for that.'

Candy has kept Jackson at arm's length since he'd ravished her in his bathroom. He drops into the salon for his usual haircut when he's home, but has been closed off, as though it never happened.

'When did he get back?'

'Last night.' Candy catches my grin.

'I see, so you've had your wild welcome home reunion? No wonder I have no muffins, you're probably feeling sleep deprived and exhausted from all that wild sex.'

'Stop!' I protest. 'I'm not giving you any details, so you can forget about all the questions on the tip of that tongue of yours.'

'Awww, damn.' Candy tries to cover the green monster that always turns up at the thought of Jackson and Skye in bed together. She should never have expected anything more from him. She had to accept it had been a slip of the tongue, a one-off. Jackson's obsession had been, and always would be, Skye.

'If you need some help shifting some boxes, I'm your girl.'

'Thanks, Candy, you're always my girl.' I hug my best friend in the whole world tightly. Candy hugs me back and gives me an extra sorry squeeze for having stepped in on my man, even though she'd never dream of telling me and knew Jackson wouldn't either.

....

JACKSON IS home when I arrive at the end of the day to pick up the things I couldn't fit into my first load this morning.

He has the rest of the barbecue chops all laid out and is cutting up sweet potato chips and a salad as I walk onto the back patio and stand awkwardly at the sliding gauzed door.

'Hey you,' I say, resisting the temptation to knock before I walk over the threshold.

'I'll be in charge of barbecue if you can work your magic with these chips,' he says.

'What you're really saying is that you want my chips prepared my way, because they're better than any other chips you've ever had?' I pick up on our long-standing chips joke.

'That's exactly what I'm saying.'

'How'd your early meeting go?'

'Good, real good. Should be up and running within a couple of weeks.'

'Wow, that's quick.'

'There's been a lot of planning for a long time, and everything's easily falling into place.'

'Have you got a name for your business?

'I have a couple of ideas. I thought I'd just keep it simple. Either Madden's Earthmoving or Groundbreakers.'

I consider the options.

'Your name has a good reputation in this area and having earth-moving in there says up front what you do. But if you want to expand then Groundbreakers might be the way to go as it's not tied to a personal name and it does give a sense of what you do. Then again, people might not figure it out so quickly.'

I usually don't give my opinion on matters like this, mostly because Jackson has never asked, and worry that I've overstepped. 'That's just my humble opinion, off the cuff.'

Jackson thinks it over.

'I dunno. I was thinking along the same lines. Maybe you could decide for me?'

I look at him in surprise. What is happening? Why is Jackson asking me to contribute to his big life decisions?

'No way, it's your decision, it's totally up to you. It's your business, you need to go with your gut on this.'

Jackson, finished with his chopping, washes his hands and comes around to where I'm sitting on the other side of the island bench.

'Thank you wise one. I've been thinking about you all day,' he says, nuzzling into my neck and running his hands over my shoulders, and down my arms before intertwining his fingers with mine.

'What's with all the bags at the front door, and the empty drawers in the bedroom?' he whispers in my ear before pulling away and moving to the fridge to get two beers out.

'Now that you're home, I was just assuming you'd want your house back. You don't need me anymore, you can manage.'

'Who says I can manage without you?'

I take a sip of my beer as he watches me intently.

'I don't want you to leave,' he says, his voice laced with emotion.

He takes a step closer until we are nose to nose. I can feel his body heat and wonder if it's my heart I can hear beating, or his.

'Stay.'

He winks at me, takes a swig of his beer and walks out to the barbecue. I stand in the kitchen confused, has he asked me to stay, or is he commanding me to stay? I feel like he expects me to fall into line with whatever he wants. Or am I overthinking it? I follow him out to the barbecue.

'I ordered the pool today,' he says.

There's no stopping you,' I laugh.

'There's no time like the present. Life's short.'

'That is true,' I reply as he hands me the tongs. 'Can you watch these for a sec? I'll go and grab the pool brochures.'

I have my back to the house, flipping the chops, when I hear him return. Expecting him to take the tongs back, I turn around to find him on one knee, holding a small black box.

'That doesn't look like a pool brochure.' My voice shakes.

'My beautiful Skye, will you please stay, and marry me?'

My face burns and I feel tears at the corner of my eyes. The moment I have dreamed of since I was a little girl, with someone down on one knee asking me to marry him, is here. Totally unexpected, totally unplanned.

I giggle nervously and take the box, opening it slowly. He remains on one knee, watching my face intently.

The cluster of diamonds around a green emerald blind me with dazzling sparkle and shine.

'I... Jackson...this is...'

I'm lost for words. Long seconds pass.

'This is the most beautiful thing I have ever seen.'

'You are the most beautiful thing I have ever seen,' Jackson says, standing slowly and stepping in close.

'Since the first moment I saw you – a young, beautiful, eighteen-year-old on the cusp of your womanhood, I have adored you. I know we didn't quite get it right the first time, but I had big ambitions and dreams. And I didn't want to tie you down when you were young and you had so much life and promise ahead of you, I wanted you to live a little.

'But since you've moved in here and all that you've done for me, and the more time I spend with you, the more time I want to spend with you. I want to spend all my time with you. I want to marry you. I want you to have my babies. I want us to live happily ever after.'

I start sobbing. He is saying everything I dreamed a man would say to me. He is everything I ever wanted. I pull the ring out of the box and slip it on my fourth finger.

'It fits perfectly,' I say between sobs.

'Of course it does. I did my homework.' Jackson pulls one of my rings out of his pocket.

'My eighteenth gift from Mum. I thought I had lost it forever!'

'I just borrowed it for a little while. I told your Mum because I knew you'd be really upset when you couldn't find it.'

I shake my head. 'I did wonder why she didn't seem as devastated as what I thought she would be when I confessed that I had lost it. You really did think of everything, that is so sweet.'

Jackson leans in and kisses tears from my cheeks before landing on my lips. I fall into his soft kiss.

Eventually we pull apart.

'So that's a yes?' Jackson asks. I look down at the ring on my finger, and for a moment it blinds me. I nod my yes, still unable to speak.

'She said yes!' Jackson yells loudly, grabbing me around the waist and twirling me around.

'Yes, yes, yes!' I laugh breathlessly.

'We're getting married!' Jackson whoops and at that exact moment the chops catch alight, and flames leap high.

'I think they're done,' I say, giggling like a schoolgirl.

...

We sit at the island bench in the kitchen, side by side eating our charred chops, Jackson twining his fingers through mine, admiring the ring he just put on my finger. We grin at each other, both laughing at our black teeth.

'Mrs Skye Madden has a very nice ring to it,' Jackson says.

'What if I want to keep my own name?' I ask.

Jackson's eyes darken. 'Why would you want to keep your own name when you can have mine?'

'Skye Tate, that's my name. That's me.'

'Yes, but if we're getting married, you're Skye Madden. You take my name because you're mine.'

My dinner threatens to come up, and I push it down. With a bubble of anger sitting in my stomach I drop the subject. I've known Jackson long enough to know this is how it was going to be. It's the way he's been brought up, as a man's man in a man's world.

Content he has won this battle, Jackson polishes off the rest of his dinner, clears our plates and leans over to kiss me for the hundredth time that night.

'I think we need to make this more official,' he says suggestively. He spins my stool to face him with one strong arm he lifts me up and carries me straight to the bedroom.

'On one condition,' I say, pushing all my doubts and fears right away.

'What's that?'

I jump out of his arms. 'You brush your teeth first!'

We stand side by side at the basin, jostling with each other to see who can brush for the longest without having to spit. I win.

When we're done Jackson shows off his perfectly straight, perfectly white teeth and I marvel as just how perfect he is from head to toe.

'There,' he says as he picks me up again like I weigh nothing. 'Let's make it official, my beautiful wife to be.'

19

SKYE

I pull into the hairdresser's car park like I do every morning before work, except this morning is different. I sit with my hand on the steering wheel for a few extra seconds, admiring the giant rock Jackson has placed on my finger.

In the light of a new day, all I can think about is how excited everybody will be at the news of Jackson and I, my first love, the perfect couple, making it official. You can always count on a small country town getting excited at an impending wedding. Not that I want to think about planning a wedding anytime soon. I just want to sit with this new idea of being engaged.

Engaged! I can't wait to see the look on Candy's face. I'd had time to go around to Mum's as well as bake muffins this morning. I was still not awake early enough to say goodbye to Jackson, who must have left before dawn. I didn't even hear him.

His note on the kitchen bench read, *Dear future Mrs Madden, see you tonight. Love from your future husband.*

He added a large cross at the bottom to seal the deal. I pushed aside the annoyance at his assumption I will take his surname, but it is not an argument I am going to have right now.

It is no surprise to Mum, of course, having been in on the lost ring situation. She shed a few tears over our early morning cuppa, sad that my temporary move out of home is permanent, but happy in the knowledge I am settling down. She is also secretly hopeful it won't be too long before the pitter patter of tiny feet and having grandchildren to spoil.

Although she would never let on, Bev thought she saw something troubled in Skye's eyes. Was it fear, doubt, concern or all of the above? Bev likes Jackson. He is a nice young man, ambitious and hard working. He will be a good provider, but he is controlling and extremely talkative.

Bev prefers the company of men who listen more than they speak. But it isn't her life. Skye has to make her own decisions, and if Skye has decided Jackson is her man, Bev will be in her corner, supporting and cheering her on.

'Skye!' Candy squeals as I walk in, adding extra volume when she spots the tray of warm muffins. 'What do we have today?'

'Today we have something extra special,' I announce. 'Poppy seed and orange muffins with passionfruit icing.'

'Passionfruit, my favourite!' Candy lifts the tea towel, admiring the icing dripping tantalisingly over the sides.

'You have really outdone yourself, Skye. What's the occasion?'

I lift my right hand and place it over my heart.

'No occasion,' I say, grinning like an idiot. Candy's screams fill every corner of the hairdressing salon as her boss and the apprentice rush over to see what the fuss is all about.

'Oh, my God. Oh, my God, you're engaged!'

Tears are streaming down Candy's cheeks and it's easy for her to pretend they are tears of joy and not tears of heartache.

She loves Skye more than life itself and swallows her jealousy, and her guilt. She is not going to let anything ruin this moment for her best friend. The moment they've talked about for years; they've shared their dreams for getting married, settling down in the town they love and living happily ever after many times.

'That is the biggest rock I have ever seen.' Candy holds my hand up and admires the way the ring sits on my finger. 'How many diamonds?'

I giggle. 'I don't know. A few. More than a few.'

'You have to tell me, how much did he spend?'

'There is no way I would ask a question like that, I have no interest in that sort of thing,' I protest.

'Well, you should,' Candy says. 'Because I can tell you that he has spent a lot on that ring. *A lot.*'

I roll my eyes. 'If you're that interested, you can ask him yourself, but I don't want to know. All I know is that it fits perfectly. I love it, and I am beyond excited to be engaged. Engaged!'

This brings on another round of squeals.

'You're going to have to just be late to work this morning. We are celebrating.' Candy disappears out the back, reappearing with a bottle of champagne and as many glasses as she can fit in one hand.

With a pop, excitement continues to bubble over and she starts pouring and handing out champagne.

She even pours a glass for old Joe, who is in for his weekly shave.

'We gather here today on this happy occasion to toast Skye and Jackson,' Candy says. Everyone repeats *Skye and Jackson* and they chink glasses and take a sip.

I float to work, and spend my day in a dream. Mrs Mac spends her day creating the biggest, most impressive bunch of flowers in secret in the back room, which she wouldn't let me enter all day.

As I lock up she appears with a large bouquet filled with every brightly-coloured flower imaginable, dominated by red, yellow and orange gerberas. There are also babies breath, white roses with the most delicious scent, native flowers, eucalyptus leaves. You couldn't imagine how perfectly they all go together, yet with her years of skill, experience and eye for colour, it is the most magical creation I have ever seen.

'You are a genius,' I say. 'So creative! You really should be selling these bouquets in Sydney, to all the rich posh people, they would love these. This is not just a bunch of flowers. This is a work of art.'

Mrs Mac blushes. 'You are the sweetest girl. It's just a few things I've thrown together.'

'I need to take some photos of this and make you up some brochures and go to Sydney myself and hand them out. I'm sure they would sell like hotcakes and you could sell them for a fortune.'

'Bless you, my girl. But enough of all that, today is your day. Stop thinking about other people and start thinking about yourself.'

'I'm going to need a truck to get this bunch of flowers home,' I laugh, struggling under its weight as I walk out the door.

'I am definitely taking photos of this as soon as I get home, and they'll be going straight into a brochure.'

'Get yourself home, quick smart, I'm sure you've got a special dinner planned.'

'Yes, we do. We're all going out for dinner at the RSL to celebrate.'

'You have a lovely time, my dear, I will see you tomorrow.'

My arms are sore by the time I get to the car, and the flowers take up the whole front seat. I admire my ring for the millionth time and breathe in the heady floral scents, wondering if maybe Mrs Skye Madden wouldn't be so bad after all.

20

SKYE

It's a home game but I've managed to get out of working the bar. Instead I'm out for a night with Jackson and Candy at the pub. The place is pumping and when the whole team walks in, freshly showered after another win in their race to the grand final, the noise levels go up a notch.

I purposely avoid scanning the crowd as they arrive, knowing Quinton will be among them. He is the last person I want to speak to. I wonder if he knows I'm engaged, I imagine he does. I rub my thumb over the base of my engagement ring for comfort. Jackson has been on my back to set a date, but there's been so many big changes and I'm deep in training for the Coolangatta again, so I keep putting him off.

I pull my hand out of Jackon's and lean in close so he can hear me. 'I'm heading to the ladies. Keep an eye on my drink? Also, keep an eye on Candy – looks like she's just about had one too many.' Jackson takes my drink as we both look over at Candy, who's flirting up a storm with the whole football team. I can't see Quinton's trademark cowboy hat amongst them, maybe he's gone home instead.

I push through the swinging doors that lead into the dark, carpeted hallway to the toilets, ladies on one side, gents on the other, when I sense someone behind me. I stop and turn, coming face to face with Quinton. Black hat, tucked in white T-shirt underneath an unbuttoned blue, white and black checked shirt, denim jeans, shiny belt buckle, polished boots.

'Hey you,' he smoulders.

'Hey yourself.' I step aside, my back to the wall, to let him pass. He stands in front of me and places a hand either side above my head. He smells like he's just out of the shower, and I notice the ends of his thick hair that curl on his neckline are slightly damp. He looks at me with the piercing, intent gaze of my fantasies.

'You're even more beautiful than I remember,' he says. I am at risk of ending up in a puddle on the floor. I part my lips and unconsciously run my tongue over my bottom lip. Everything around us – the smell of smoke wafting through from the bar, the urine soaked into the paint and tiles of the old pub toilets, the chatter and music from outside – disappears.

I am trembling, and my heart beats rapidly. No, I can't, it would be so wrong. My thumb goes to the base of my engagement ring. My life is all planned out.

I duck my head and walk into the ladies. Quinton follows. I turn to tell him to leave but I have no words. He pins me to the wall, and I shift my hands to his chest to feel his strong, beating heart. 'What's that aftershave you're wearing?' I whisper.

'I'm not sure, just something I found in the cupboard.' He is so close I can smell the malt of the beer he's just drunk. He looks down at my hands, then back into my eyes.

'What's that ring you're wearing?' he asks without words. I don't look away but drop my hands from his chest.

'I'm engaged.'

He doesn't break my gaze and leans closer, reaching for my hands and intertwining his fingers with mine. I am hypnotised and fall into his spell.

'You should wait, you're too young,' he whispers into my ear, breathing hot air that is doing wicked things to my body.

A loud bang as someone pushes open the swinging doors breaks the moment, followed quickly by the familiar voice of Candy, three sheets to the wind.

'Well, well, well, what is going on in here? I think you're in the wrong bathroom buddy,' she says to the back of Quinton, not realising his broad shoulders and large biceps are hiding her best friend.

He moves aside.

'Skye? Quinton?' A look I don't recognise passes across Candy's face. Is it disappointment? Disapproval? Surely not. Candy isn't like that.

'Looks like I've interrupted something important,' she says stiffly.

'No, you haven't. Quinton is just leaving,' I say, my eyes boring into his. His face set, he turns and walks out, leaving Candy and I alone. Before she can say any more, I follow him out.

Candy finds me back with Jackson, snuggled in tight, holding his hand, laughing and smiling as if less than five minutes ago, I hadn't been pinned up against the wall with the most gorgeous cowboy Candy had ever laid eyes.

Her green-eyed monster rears its ugly head at the fact she is nothing but a good time girl, an 'on the side'. She wants the massive white wedding, the status of being a wife – the things Skye is about to have. The choices here are limited, and any eligible bachelor is well and truly taken. She walks over to stand on the other side of Jackson, plastering a fake smile on her face.

'Another drink, Candy?' he asks.

'Sure. Why not?'

Jackson leaves to get another round, leaving the two girls alone. Silence stretches between them.

'It's not what you think,' I say.

'I'm not thinking anything.'

I hear the hardness in her tone.

'Quinton is fully taken. Me too. That's what I was telling him, about the engagement.'

'I heard his girlfriend left him,' Candy snaps. 'That's the rumor around town, anyway.'

'Oh.' I wonder if she realises her words have hit me in the heart.

'I thought you'd know that.'

'No, I know she's not there much, but she's never really been there. That doesn't mean she's left him. She's a hot shot lawyer with a busy job. Last I knew she has been convalescing at the farm after her accident. A fair bit of time has passed, and I figure she'd be better by now and back at work.' My words gush out as I over explain.

'Anyway,' Candy leans in close. 'You know I love you, and you're my best friend in the whole world, but I wouldn't like to see Jackson get hurt in all of this.'

'Nobody's going to get hurt because there's nothing between me and Quinton. That ship has sailed, well and truly,' I reply.

'What's this about a sailing ship? Something about loose lips sink ships perhaps?' Jackson asks, as he hands Candy a drink, sensing tension between the two friends. He glares at Candy and she glares right back. I don't notice, as I've just caught Quinton's eyes on us and by the time I rejoin the conversation, Candy and Jackson are both looking into their drinks.

I scull mine. 'I'm ready to go home,' I say to Jackson.

'Whatever you want, baby. Here Candy, you can have mine.'

I grab Jackson's hand and pull him behind me as I walk quickly out the door.

'See you Candy, have a good night,' I call out, wondering where this wedge between us has stemmed from. If only I knew. If I did, it wouldn't be Jackson I'm going home with tonight, that's for sure.

...

I START WORKING on Jackson as soon as he starts the car, and by the time we get home I have removed my underwear and he has a hard-on ready to burst.

. . .

WITH LIPS LOCKED and pulling at each other's clothes in a passionate frenzy, we almost fall over the threshold at the back door. He lifts me onto the island bench and finger fucks me while kissing my neck before lifting me off to carry me to the loungeroom. My feminine touch is everywhere. New plants, cushions, pretty smells, pictures on the wall, photo frames of our younger years, faces smiling from the hallway table.

I PULL off his shirt and in our kissing tangle, Jackson knocks a framed photo off the table.

WE BOTH STOOP down at the same time to pick it up.

'REMEMBER THAT NIGHT?' Jackson asks, as he places the photo of Candy and I drunk as skunks on the couch as one of his house parties when we were eighteen.

'I SURE DO. BEST NIGHT EVER.' I reply, kissing him fervently, my hands all over his muscly chest.

'Are you sure you remember it? You were pretty wasted,' Jackson says. Even though our school years are far behind us, Jackson still pictures us as we were back then.

'I remember most of it. Not all of it.' I falter. We pull apart. I don't want to talk about that night. Every time Jackson mentions it I pretend I was too drunk to remember. But I remember every bit of it, including the way it made me feel to see Jackson fucking Candy right in front of me.

'Want another drink?' he asks, as he looks around the lounge-room which was a far cry from the bachelor's pad lounge of that night long ago. He can't wait to fill this room with children's toys. Jackson hands me a brandy and dry and chooses a record.

'ABBA. I love this album,' I say with delight as I take the cover, trying to get my head out of the past and back into right now. 'I thought they were so cool in their white suits with their white helicopter. When I was a little girl, I wanted to be ABBA.'

'I bet you those four got up for some kinky things,' Jackson says, his mind on a single track after the way Skye had ravaged him on the way home. She'd taken things to a whole new level of excitement, and he wanted more.

'Wouldn't that be fun? A foursome.' He pulls me close and kisses me fully on the lips.

'Got anyone in mind?' I reply, happy to go along with some fantasy conversation, as long as it is just conversation, as long as it is just a fantasy.

'How about the two girls from ABBA, you and me?'

'Now, that could be fun.' I close my eyes as Jackson kisses me and lifts my shirt over my head. He takes his mouth off my lips and moves down my neck and to my breasts.

'Do you reckon they'd be into it?'

I arch my back in pleasure as he devours me. 'I'm sure they would.'

He pulls my short denim skirt off and kneels so he can look at my smooth lips. He gently parts them, twirling his fingers around, teasing me until I am begging him to touch the sweet spot. I grab behind his head and push him into me so I can feel the flick of his tongue along my clit.

He resists, then stands to kiss me.

'Tell me what you want,' he orders.

'You know what I want. I want you.'

'That's what you're going to get,' Jackson growls, taking his jeans off, then pushing me down to kneel so he can put his hard cock into my mouth.

When he's about to burst Jackson pushes me away and lifts me up, throwing me roughly on the couch.

'Spread your legs, wide,' he orders as he kneels on the couch and lifts my hips up to plunge his tongue deep inside my moist, throbbing lips. He pulls his tongue out and moves up to kiss me.

'Taste yourself,' he says. 'And imagine it's you with your tongue between Frida's legs, licking her out, while I fuck you from behind.'

I groan into his mouth, and he thrusts into me, before pulling out. He stands beside my head and I move onto my side so he can fuck my mouth again. I lick my wetness off his cock, and he chokes me.

I feel him harden, and I reach up to cup his balls. Jackson moans with pleasure. 'Slow, slow, slower,' he says as I suck him off. I ignore him and pull him closer into me until I can hardly breathe. I pull my mouth off and circle his tip with my tongue. 'Choke me, come inside my mouth,' I say just as I suck him hard and push him in deep.

Unable to contain himself, Jackson's cum dribbles out the side of my mouth as I can't swallow quickly enough.

He flops down on the couch and hands me a box of tissues from the side table. As I wipe, I hear a faint snore. I stand, feeling partly satisfied, partly resentful. Maybe it's the early morning starts and all the pressure of getting his business started. Maybe it's him. Maybe it's me.

I turn away, a mix of emotions, and the snores get louder. I stand under the hot shower, eyes closed, with two fingers inside me while I rub my clit with my other hand, wondering if the ABBA fantasy will finish me off. Quinton appears behind my eyes, staring at me intently from underneath his cowboy hat in the pub toilets while I rest my hands on his chest, and I instantly come, panting and whimpering as I imagine what it would feel like to have him inside me, every day of the week and five times on Sundays.

21

SKYE

I wait patiently at the bar, which is ten cowboys deep. It feels like every cowboy in Australia is here for one of the biggest rodeo events Scone has ever put on.

I'd left Candy beside the ring, chatting up a group of cowboys who'd made a beeline for us as soon as they spotted our tight, bejeweled jeans, skimpy white tops and matching white hats.

'We've got to stop meeting like this,' a familiar voice breathes heavily into my ear from behind.

I turn to be nose to nose with Quinton.

'You mean at a bar?'

'Just meeting in general. At the footy. At the pub, and now at a rodeo. Since when are you a rodeo queen?' He steps back to look me up and down and that familiar thrill that only he gives me runs from my head to my toes.

'I know a lot more about cowboys than what you think,' I reply, turning back to the bar. Who does he think he is flirting with me when it is very clear that not only am I not available, but also not interested?

It takes a lot of effort to hate this man, and I work hard at it as I try and remain loyal in my actions and my thoughts, to Jackson.

My latest conclusion, especially after that night at the pub and rumours around town that he's going home with a different girl every weekend now his girlfriend has left, is he is no different to the rest of the cowboys I know. I had built him up to be something exotic and unique but realise he isn't. He's just another cowboy more interested in looking after his animals than his women.

'How have you been?' he asks.

'How do you think I've been? Not that you care.'

'What do you mean?'

All my pent-up frustration and hurt while my life hurtles away from me comes out. I turn to him, my eyes spitting fire.

'What do I mean? What do you care how I've been when you shoved me aside like a used car when it didn't suit you to have me around because you were trying to save your precious relationship? Which was obviously not that precious to you, judging by the fact you try and get your hands down my pants every time you see me.'

I watch Quinton flush under my piercing gaze.

'I had a bit going on at the time, I didn't always make the right choices.'

I ignore his comment, I'm not finished.

'You waltz in and take over this business that I have worked at since I was sixteen years old. You make me fall for you with all your gentlemanly cowboy manners and make out you're such a nice bloke with a broken heart that needed someone to help fix you.

'And I fell madly, deeply in love with you, thinking we were meant to be together. But when it didn't suit you anymore, you dropped me like a hot cake.'

'It wasn't like that,' he says softly.

I turn my back again as the line shuffles closer.

'It was exactly like that,' I reply. Quinton moves closer and puts his hand on my waist. I can smell the mix of sweat, dust his woody aftershave which I've been trying to erase from my memory.

'I didn't mean to hurt you,' he says.

I don't move for a few seconds, enjoying the familiar comfort of his large frame engulfing my petite size six, and don't let on my disappointment when he moves his hand off my waist.

'Here with your boyfriend?' he asks, moving up so we're side by side.

'Not my boyfriend. My fiancé. And no, I'm not here with him, I'm here with Candy. He's away for work.'

'Where does he work?'

I look at him quizzically.

'I thought you would have done a bit more research and know all about him.' Quinton shrugs his shoulders. 'Why would I feel the need to research your boyfriend, I mean fiancé? I'm not interested in him.'

We shuffle towards the bar in silence.

'So, you're getting married, 'ay,' Quinton says, looking down at the sparkling rock on my finger.

Yes, yes, I am.'

'Set a wedding date?'

'No, not yet. It's all happened a bit fast, and Jackson has started a new business, and he's really busy, and I'm really busy, and so we just haven't talked about a date yet.'

'I hear you're getting married to your high school sweetheart?'

'Who told you that? That he was my high school sweetheart?'

'I dunno, probably the boys at footy training.' Quinton tries to act nonchalant.

'So you *have* researched him.'

'No I haven't. I have just picked up a few threads here and there.'

'I wouldn't call us high school sweethearts. I first met him when I was in high school but he wasn't in high school. He's older, then he moved away for work and things fizzled out. He bought a house in town and needed someone to house sit for him while he was away. I was living there for, I don't know, maybe a year, and then he finished up with his job and came back to start a new business. And as you know, the rest is history.' I finish in a rush and wave my hand around. The diamond glitters in Quinton eyes.

We shuffle closer to the bar.

'In case you didn't hear me the first time, I'm sorry that I hurt you,' Quinton says awkwardly.

It is on the tip of my tongue to reassure him it was fine, that he hadn't hurt me, but there is something about Quinton that allows me to be fully truthful.

'You did really hurt me. You shouldn't have been with me while you were still so wrapped up in Beth,' I scold, my eyes wide.

'I know,' Quinton says, his tone regretful. 'I know I did the wrong thing by you and by Beth. I'm an arsehole, through and through.'

'Yes, you were an arsehole, but you're not being an arsehole right now. Takes a lot for a man to say he's sorry, especially a cowboy.' I smile gently.

We've reached the bar and I order two beers then look at Quinton. 'What would you like?'

'I'll have a XXXX,' he says to the barmaid. I go to pay, but he pushes my money aside, handing over a fifty dollar bill. 'My shout.'

'Oh, you're a nice cowboy,' the girl behind the bar winks at him. 'You're one lucky girl having a nice, hot cowboy buy your drinks.'

'He's not nice,' I return. 'He's an arsehole.' Quinton chuckles and winks back at the barmaid. 'I am nice, she just hasn't seen that side of me yet.'

'I'd better get back to Candy,' I say, as I slide Candy's beer into my back pocket.

Quinton takes my can and opens it, then hands it back to me. He opens his and lifts it to mine.

'Cheers,' he says.

'Cheers,' I say, a cheeky smile spreading across my face. '...to the ninth cowboy that's bought me a drink tonight.'

I walk off, feeling his eyes on me. I exaggerate the swing of my hips and hope he's getting a good look. If he is going to flirt with me every time I see him, who am I not to lap it all up?

'That didn't take long,' Candy groans as she retrieves the beer out of my back pocket.

'The bar is ten deep. Where's all your cowboys gone?'

'We can do better than them. They were a bunch of childish little boys.'

'We? I'm not here to score, Candy. I've got a perfectly good fiancé, remember. Who is working his arse off to keep me in the manner I am learning to grow and love.'

Candy takes an awkward sip from her can. Moments like these, when it is just her and Skye in best friend mode, she feels like a piece of dirt for what she is doing with her best friend's fiancé.

As the night wears on the crowd gets louder and drunker. Candy is drinking like a fish. I'm the designated driver so I've only had the one beer Quinton bought.

Once all the bull and horse jumping finishes, we move into the bar where a band is set up on the edge of a portable dance floor. Lee Kernaghan is rocking out our favourite tunes from *The Outback Club* to *Boys from the Bush* and our all-time favourite, *Country Girls*.

A mechanical bull creates plenty of merriment, and during a band break, Candy, who's as drunk as a skunk, climbs up. I'm in hysterics watching her and will be of no help whatsoever if she falls. After one small buck she does fall, her beautiful full breasts tumbling out of her skimpy top and getting the attention of every bloke in the cheering crowd.

Not to be deterred, she climbs up again, giving the growing crowd a wonderous look at her generous arse, which they all want a piece of as they watch it moving up and down in the saddle.

'Go Candy, hang on girl,' I call out, cheering and clapping as she expertly hugs her legs in and maintains the perfect balance.

'She's got a good seat in the saddle,' I hear from behind me.

Over the raucous crowd I don't recognise it's Quinton until I turn around.

'Yes, she has always been a natural on a horse. She never had one of her own. Her Mum could never afford it. But if anyone was built to be a cowgirl, it's Candy.'

Like every male within close proximity, Quinton can't tear his eyes off Candy on her bucking bull.

'How long have you and Candy been friends?' he asks.

'Forever. We used to do everything together, but not so much these days. You know, life gets busy. People drift apart.'

'She looks like she's a lot of fun,' Quinton says. I looked at him sharply, an unexpected shiver of jealousy taking my breath away.

'She *is* a lot of fun,' I say, as the thought runs through my mind about whether Quinton has ever gone home with Candy after a drunken night at the pub. I quickly push it aside. Of course he hasn't. Where did that thought even come from? Candy knows how I felt about Quinton, and even though I was with Jackson, she'd know Quinton was too close to home and hence off limits. It is an unspoken rule between us.

'All eyes are on her, and I reckon a few of the lads are wondering if they're in with a chance, but she's not the prettiest girl at the rodeo,' Quinton continues. I turn to him and he gently tips my chip upwards. 'She's right here.' He leans down and gently kisses my cheek. Instinctively my hands go to his waist and I move closer. His lips land softly on mine and for the briefest second I give in to the warmth and safety of his kiss.

Reluctantly I pull away. 'I'm sorry, Quinton. I can't.'

He shrugs his shoulders and turns back to Candy, who at that moment loses concentration and lands on the ground with a thud. Quinton jumps over the ring like the true gentleman he is, and helps her to her feet.

'Why thank you, hunky cowboy who's come to rescue me.' She loops her arms around his neck and leans into him as he leads her over to me. She collapses into my arms, giggling drunkenly.

'I wish I had a horse, a real horse,' she says.

'Maybe one day you will,' I laugh.

'Your lovely Quinton came to rescue me,' Candy says.

'He's not my Quinton,' I say sharply. Infuriatingly he winks at me. Candy misses the whole thing and continues on her drunken rave.

'Maybe you could have the lovely Quinton, and I could have the lovely Jackson.'

'Okay Candy Mandy, time to get those wobbly boots off and take you home I think,' I say.

'No!' she protests. 'Take me to the bar or take me to the dance floor but don't take me home, I'm having way too much fun.'

Candy trips and Quinton catches her before she hits the ground again.

'I'm definitely taking you home. Thank you, Quinton – it's good to see you but we're out of here.' I struggle to hold Candy up as we walk towards the carpark and again Quinton comes to the rescue. He lifts her like she's as light as a feather, which she isn't, especially when she's drunk.

'You lead the way, Skye,' he says as Candy wraps her arms around his neck and nuzzles into him.

'I love cowboys,' she murmurs. 'Save a horse, ride a cowboy. I love riding horses, and I love riding cowboys. Maybe you could take me for a ride, on your horse that is.'

When we get to the car I go around to the driver's side to unlock, and Candy continues her drunken conversation in Quinton's ear. 'I'm an awful best friend,' she whispers. 'The worst kind. I'm sleeping with Jackson, my best friend's fiancé. What sort of slut am I to do that to the most beautiful friend in the world...'

Quinton puts his fingers to her lips and when I am back to open the passenger door I hear him saying 'Shhh, it's okay, Skye is going to take you home.' He looks at me with a strange expression I can't read. 'You right to drive? Given that the beer I shouted was your ninth beer from a cowboy?'

'Haha, I'm right as rain. That wasn't my ninth, it was my first, and my last. Candy always hits it pretty hard at rodeos so I always drive. There's a few cowboys here with bad reputations and I never want her to end up waking up in the morning after having someone, or more than one, take advantage of her.'

There's that strange expression again from Quinton. 'That's thoughtful of you,' he says stiffly. 'She's lucky to have a friend like you to look out for her.'

'Are you right for a lift home? You can jump in the back if you want?'

'Nah, I'm good. I'm here with Austin, he's kicking around somewhere.'

'Austin! I haven't seen him for ages and didn't realise he was here.'

'He's hard to catch these days, he's got a new girlfriend. We came on a double date, actually, but my date ditched me after about an hour. I mustn't have been stimulating enough for her.'

'A date? I did hear you were back on the market but wasn't sure if it was town gossip,' I say bravely, wanting him to confirm or deny the rumours.

'I guess. Whole new world for me. Not doing too well either. Haven't dated anyone in a long time.'

I bite back all my questions. I'm not one to listen to gossip, but it seems the rumours Candy shared with me about Beth are true.

'You've got a fair bit of competition here; you're not the only cowboy in the stadium.'

'I reckon I'm probably the only *real* cowboy.'

'Maybe so. Not that anyone would know, you're so quiet. Buckle bunnies like a real cowboy, but if you don't put yourself out there, they won't even know you're here.'

'I see. So to find myself a nice girl I need to change who I am? I don't think I'll bother.'

My knees go weak.

'You know what we were talking about at the bar earlier?' he says, moving closer. 'It was a confusing time. I had bitten off more than I could chew. You know, starting the farm, making that big financial and personal commitment with Beth. I was out of my comfort zone on every level.'

'I can relate to that.' I nod in agreeance, trying to ignore the heady smell of his pine centered aftershave mixed with dust and sweat from a warm day at the rodeo.

'I thought I knew what I was doing,' he continued, but in actual fact, I was winging it in every corner and...' Quinton falters.

'Go on,' I urge, not wanting him to stop, 'you can be honest with me.'

'Well, I thought Beth and I wanted the same things, and it was hard to admit that we didn't. Maybe we never really did.'

I take a deep breath and get brave. 'Where's Beth now?'

'In Sydney. Where she's always wanted to be.'

'So, it really is over between you two?'

'Yeah, it's been over for a while now.'

'I see. I'm glad it's a long time ago, because I've heard a lot of rumours about you and the girls around the footy club. I'm not one for believing or spreading town talk, but there's some humdingers floating around.'

Quinton looks at his feet, and I notice a flush around his collar.

'Beth was my first love, and I truly, madly, deeply loved her with every part of my being. I tried, I really did, but she found out about us and it was all over.'

'She found out about us? Did you tell her?'

'No I didn't,' Quinton looks into my eyes. 'I should've, but I didn't. Instead, she found a condom and your black G-string in the spare room, not long after she got home from the hospital.'

It's my turn to flush. I'd left in such a hurry that night, I didn't realise the condom I had in my pants pocket had dropped out. I did wonder where my G-string ended up but figured Quinton found it and disposed of it appropriately.

I'm conscious of getting Candy home, but I don't want this conversation to end.

'Once I realised it was over for good, I went a bit mad,' he continues. 'You know, the rumours, they're probably not all true, but I had a lot of drunken nights and no shortage of attention.'

'It's the hat. The jeans. The boots. The belt. Irresistible combo,' I say softly. 'Where are you at now?'

'Nowhere really, the whole *save a horse ride a cowboy* doesn't really suit me. One-night stands are not my sort of thing.'

'That's definitely not what I heard,' I say.

'You know what small towns are like. You shouldn't believe everything you hear.'

'I know, can't let the truth get in the way of a good story.'

The silence stretches between us, but I don't want to break this magic bubble we've found ourselves in.

'Well, I better get Candy home. She's going to have a very sore head tomorrow.'

'She sure is. She's lucky to have a friend like you.'

'She's my best friend, my best friend in the whole wide world. I'd do anything for her. We all need a best friend.'

Quinton looks as though he's about to say something, but stops.

'What about you? Have you made some good mates?' I ask.

'A few, footy's been good for that. Also got one of my mates from boarding school working out at the farm for a few months, giving me a hand. He's got a bit of a passion for pastures and I've put him in charge of that side of things while I focus on the sheds.'

'That's a good mix,' my eyes light up. 'I like to hear you're still focused on getting those soils right.'

'I think you were there in the early days talking about all this excess manure, so I'm really trying to utilise it on on the farm and get everything all working together. I've also enrolled in a permaculture course. I thought it might give me some new ideas seemings I know fuck all about pig farming.'

'Don't sell yourself short, Quinton. You've got a natural instinct, you'll figure it out.'

I made no attempt to move, enjoying being so close I can feel the heat of him.

'You're easy to talk to, you know that? I miss having you out on the farm to talk ideas over with.'

Instinctively my thumb goes to the back of my engagement ring and twists it around. What am I thinking? I step back, breaking the magic threads between us. I have no business standing here in the half dark, leaning up against the car, nose to nose with the man of my fantasies.

A knock on the window interrupts us. 'Skye Pie, what are you doing? Let's go back to the bar.'

'Gotta go, before she escapes. See you round, Quinton.'

'Yeah, see you round.'

I watch Quinton from the inside of the car as he swaggers away and disappears into the crowd of cowboy hats and belt buckles. Timing is everything. Quinton is free, and available. I'm not free, and engaged. We're obviously not meant to be.

...

The next morning Candy, who I half carried half dragged from the car to the spare room, finds me in the garden.

With bleary eyes and her blonde, curly hair poking in all directions, she flops on the grass next to the new garden bed I'm weeding and preparing for planting.

'What a night,' Candy says, her voice husky and hung over. 'I had no idea where I was when I woke up in a strange house, in a bed all by myself. I was sure a hot cowboy took me home.'

'You're partly right, a hot cowboy did carry you to the car.'

Candy giggles. 'That's what I remember. Not just any cowboy, *your* hot cowboy – Quinton! Yes, he's the last thing I remember, carrying me in his big strong arms underneath that brooding black hat of his. I thought all my Christmases had come at once.'

'He was a true gentleman, as per usual, and didn't take advantage. You were in quite the state.'

'Must've been when I switched from the beers to the bourbon. I'm a bit sore too, and there's a massive bruise on my bum.'

'That's from falling off the bull.'

'What bull?'

'The mechanical bucking bull. First attempt was pretty lame and you only lasted a couple of seconds. Second attempt was much more successful.'

Candy lays one her back, covering her eyes with her arm. 'That sunshine is way too bright.'

'It's a pretty good day, perfect for gardening.'

Candy groans. 'You and your boring gardening. What are you planting today?'

'Native grasses along with a row of bottlebrushes – red ones – to bring a few more birds in. This whole area I'm turning into a native garden. The original garden was mostly roses and more of an English theme, but while I want to preserve some of it from a historical perspective, I want to make it more Australian.'

'What is it about gardening that you love so much?'

'I don't know. I just like getting my hands dirty, I guess. And I love watching things grow, I love finding the right spots for plants and seeing them flourish. I love how everything all comes together, then the birds come in and the butterflies.'

'Enough garden talk, you big plant nerd,' Candy says as she sits up and slowly gets to her feet. 'Want to go out for brunch? I'm hungry.'

'I can cook you something here?' I say, dusting off my hands.

'No, you've gone to enough trouble for me already. How about we go down to the Belmore for some hot chips with barbecue sauce and malted milk milkshakes?'

'Sounds good,' I say, I'll just pack up here and meet you inside.'

'I'll just wait in the car for you,' Candy says, reluctant to go back into the house which holds memories of her and Jackson in every room. From him laying her out on the timber floorboards in the wide hallway to eat her out, or stripping her naked in the spare room and tying her to the bed head so he has complete control and dominance while he fucks her from every angle. Although she vowed that time with him in the bathroom was a one and only, every time he calls she turns her world inside out to get to him.

Sitting across from each other at the pub, I reach over to hold Candy's hands in mine.

'I had fun going to the rodeo with you,' I say. 'We haven't been hanging out enough lately.'

'No, we haven't. You're far too busy for me these days,' Candy says.

I hug her extra tight as we say our goodbyes in the street. 'No matter how busy life gets, you'll always be my best Candy Mandy. I love you.'

Candy doesn't answer, and as she turns to leave I see tears in her eyes and vow to make more of an effort to spend time with her, so we can get back to the way we were.

22

SKYE

I leave work early to grab a shower and get changed into something more official looking for a photo shoot with the local paper about the community garden Bev and I started, which has now expanded into a community pantry.

The local council, after Mrs Mac urged me to put in an application, has given money to employ me two days a week to manage the pantry where people can buy fresh produce, donated goods and excess items from the supermarket for no set cost, just whatever they can afford.

Donations from supermarkets and local gardeners, along with what grows in the community garden, keeps the shelves stocked with fresh produce. Quinton is one of the locals who donates, and he and Austin come in as volunteers to the community garden as well.

Quinton and I are more comfortable around each other, with my focus more and more on my future with Jackson. We've set a wedding date for next autumn, my favourite time of year, not too hot, not too cold, with the deep, earthy colours of the turning leaves. Mrs Mac has already started planning the bouquets and I have asked Candy to be my one and only bridesmaid, dressed in a deep rust colour that will match Jackson and his best man's ties and cummerbunds and be set off by their pale cream suits.

I have big plans for the garden and pantry too. It seems I can't stop planning, now that I've found my true passion. I want to set up a coffee shop and the RSL has granted me the use of their commercial kitchen outside of lunch and dinner prep and service, so I can run cooking classes for people who have never been taught how to grow, store or cook healthy foods.

It ticks all my boxes for making my country community better. I love working with the volunteers, managing the garden, bringing in other experts like local chefs and reducing the amount of food that gets wasted. It is a feel-good project on every level.

Since the rodeo, Quinton and I have avoided deep conversations or references to complicated feelings. He seems to accept, and respect, that my future is with Jackson. I do catch him looking at me wistfully every now and then but I push away any feelings he brings up, confident in the commitment I have made to Jackson.

Ah, Jackson. His earthmoving business, or should I say, our earth-moving business, has become so successful that I barely see him. He works long days and into the night. Some nights he doesn't get home until midnight, too exhausted to talk, let alone anything else. I don't mind so much, I've parked my desires and diverted all that energy into other things, like the community garden and this all-consuming community pantry project.

I enter via the back door, past the new pool which I've landscaped around in a semi-tropical theme with golden cane and cocos palms, dumping everything on the island bench in the kitchen before walking towards the bedroom.

The bedroom door is shut.

That's odd, I think to myself. Maybe Jackson is having a sleep. A shiver of worry about how hard he's working runs through me. He is raking in the money, has bought more machines and is getting more work than he can handle. The pressures of employing people, meeting deadlines, putting in new tenders and fixing fuck-ups seems to be getting to him.

I quietly push the door open so I don't wake him. At that exact moment I hear a scream. The curtains are drawn and the room is pitch dark, so I flip on a light, only to be greeted by the image of Candy sitting on Jackson's face while he licks her vigorously, making her scream as she climaxes.

In slow motion, I take in tiny details. Red marks on the soft white cheeks of Candy's peach shaped arse from where Jackson has slapped and gripped her tight. Candy's clothes strewn all over the floor, from the door to the bed, a trail that tells the story of Jackson being impatient to get them off. Two of his neck ties knotted around the timber bedhead, which I imagine are intended for Candy, most likely after he finishes eating her.

Lost in the throes of ecstasy, it takes Candy a moment to register what is happening. As soon as she realises she hurriedly moves off Jackson's face and runs into the bathroom, leaving his lips, nose and chin covered in sticky cum. I walk calmly into the walk-in robe and retrieve a neatly-folded and ironed hanky I had put on his underwear shelf the other day.

'How long?' I say, my eyes flashing as I hand it to him.

Candy reappears, dressed and pleading.

'I'm so sorry, Skye, I'm sorry,' she says, over and over.

I turn to look into her eyes, with mine so dark they're almost black.

'How long? How long has this been going on behind my back?'

Neither of them answer. Candy is reduced to hysterical sobbing and Jackson is sitting on the edge of the bed, still naked, with his head in his hands.

I return slowly to the walk-in robe and select clean underwear and the clothes I plan to wear to the photo shoot. I carry them into the bathroom.

The tears come while I watch shampoo and my carefully curated future, my hopes, my dreams, my whole fucking life, go down the drain. By the time I've finished showering, small pieces are starting to fall into place. Little moments, conversations, comments and innuendos that I shook off at the time. I'm such an idiot, I was blind to it all.

I know Candy inside out, and although I can't believe what she's done to me, I'm not surprised. Mum always encouraged me to be cautious; since we were young girls in primary school, Candy had always wanted what I had. Back then it was my coloured pencils and new sneakers. Now it was much more serious.

By the time I am showered, dressed, my hair blow-dried and makeup on, I have pulled myself together. I march out of the bathroom with clear purpose and courage driven by red hot rage. The bed is made, the ties are gone and there is not a thing out of place.

I find Jackson at the kitchen table, his head still in his hands, fully clothed. Candy is nowhere in sight.

'Skye,' he stands up quickly and tries to grab my arm.

'Stop,' I cut him off as I twist my sparkling, shiny, over the top, meaningless engagement ring off my finger. 'I have a very important photo shoot with the paper to go to, remember that? My big day today. Obviously not important enough for you to set aside any time for, given that you're so fucking busy with your business, and your *business*.'

'But we need to talk. I need to explain,' he pleads.

'I don't want to hear anything you have to say. What can you say? I'm not interested in your excuses.'

I finally get the ring off, step back, take a moment to get my aim right and throw it. I watch it hit his forehead before it bounces onto the table, leaving a deep cut. Small droplets of blood form and start to trickle towards his eyebrows.

'There is nothing to explain. The situation is pretty clear. So take your fucking gawdy piece of shit engagement ring and shove it up Candy's arse.'

23

SKYE

After wearing a fake smile for two hours, having fake cheerful conversations with all the excited people who'd gathered for the launch of the new community pantry, I race to my car. Several people ask after Jackson, who was wise enough not to show up. As soon as I get behind the wheel, sobs rack my body. I blubber and hiccup my way around the streets of Scone and aimlessly drive, not knowing where to go or what to do. I end up a few kilometres out of town, on the road to Quinton's, to one of my favorite hideaways by Dart Brook Creek.

Once my hysteria has subsided, I am weary and heartsore. How could they? How long has this been going on without me knowing? How long has Jackson been telling me he loves me, adores me, and can't wait to walk down the aisle with me, while going behind my back with my best friend in the whole world? My mind rakes over every conversation, every interaction between the three of us, since Jackson got down on one knee and proposed by the barbecue.

I have been so blind, self-assured and confident that Jackson and I are the perfect couple, about to embark on the perfect happy life in my perfect hometown. Despite Quinton lurking in the deep, dark, hidden corners of my mind, and making my heart skip a beat every time we crossed paths, I have never seriously contemplated walking away from the future I was building with Jackson since our engagement.

Then it hits me. Karma. *The sum of a person's actions in this and previous states of existence, viewed as deciding their fate in future existences.* More simply, *what goes around comes around.* This is my karma. I deserve this after what I did to Beth. I felt guilt but I never actually thought about how she would feel if she found out what Quinton and I had done.

I attempt to reassure myself, *they weren't engaged.* Deep down I know that's irrelevant. They were committed to each other, they were building a future together. I stepped in without a thought apart from the thoughts of what I wanted to do with Quinton, what I believed he wanted to do with me.

A chill in the air settles on my bare arms as the sun slowly descends towards the horizon. Twittering birds finish their conversations for the day, in preparation for darkness when their trills and chattering cease for the night.

It's rained recently, so the creek is running and bubbling. Water passes over rocks and skims around logs and the constant flow calms me. Eventually the sniffing, hiccupping, sad-girl noises coming from my body disappear.

It's almost dark. Anger courses through my veins, guilt not far behind to remind me I am also a bad person, even if I try and pretend I'm not. I slowly uncurl myself and stand, dusting the leaves and sticks from my bum before striding purposefully back to my car. I know exactly what I need to do, but first, I need to find a safe place to regroup.

...

I LET myself in quietly via the back door. She is sitting at the kitchen table about to start eating her dinner.

'Skye,' she looks up, startled, 'what are you doing here?'

Tears bubbling dangerously close to the surface threaten to spill.

'I'm wondering if I can sleep here the night, Mum.'

'Of course, love. What's happened? Is everything okay?' She puts her knife and fork down and goes to stand. I motion for her to stay seated. She ignores me and already has a second place set and is at the bench serving up mashed potatoes, homemade rissoles and peas before I can say another word.

'No, everything's not okay, but I really don't want to talk about it.' My voice cracks.

'Here,' she says gently. 'Sit down. Have some dinner. You look terrible. You're so pale. You left the community pantry so quickly, I didn't know where you'd gone.'

'Thanks, Mum, but I'm not hungry. Maybe I'll eat something later. If you don't mind, I might just go and have a shower and hop into bed.'

Mum wraps me in a warm, motherly hug, and I breathe in her familiar scent; a mixture of garden soil, rissoles and her musky perfume.

'Okay, love, I'll be up for a while. Let me know if you need anything.'

Snuggled in my childhood bed in a pair of old pyjamas that didn't make the move to Jackson's house, I pull the doona over my head, trying to block out the light.

I squeeze my eyes tight shut, hoping darkness will envelop me and help me forget I have just lost two of my most important people. It is exhaustion that finally plunges me into the darkness I crave, and it is only then that I can find peace, however brief it might be, from the disaster my life has become.

...

. . .

I have been lying awake for hours before I hear the familiar sounds of Mum's early morning routine. For as long as I can remember she's up before five, ready to pack more into her day than what most people can pack into a week. When I hear her tea-making sounds, I pat out to the kitchen in my fluffy bed socks, looking as much like the zombie that I feel.

She knows me well enough not to pepper me with questions, and it isn't until she pours our second cup from the large tea pot in the centre of the table that I am ready to speak.

'Would you mind if I move back home for a short while?' I ask softly. 'I understand you're probably glad to have the space to yourself and be rid of me, so it won't be forever. It's just until I find a place of my own.'

'Of course, you can come back! It's very quiet without you, and there's been more than one occasion where I've had to resist picking up the phone and call you because I miss our dinner chats and watching the Gilmore Girls together on the couch.'

'Oh, Mum, I didn't realise you were lonely. I thought you'd have Bill around here every night, giving you company!'

'He is here, sometimes,' Mum grins, 'but I'm not ready to let a man mess up my routine and mess up my space. I've lived without a man in my house for a very long time, and I quite like it that way.'

'Looks like I'm going to have to get used to living without a man,' I say softly. Mum waits patiently.

'The engagement is off. We're done.'

Mum gasps. 'Off? So suddenly? What happened?'

Tears prick at the corner of my eyes. I am unsure if I want to divulge the truth. It feels so shameful and dirty to speak out loud. All of a sudden I'm ravenous, I get up to make myself some toast. With my back turned, as I watch the hot tiny toaster bars change the colour of my multi-grain bread from brown to dark brown, I find the words.

'I found Jackson and Candy together.'

'What do you mean together?'

'I mean together *together*, in my bed, in my house, together.'

'Oh, love, I'm so sorry.' Mum wraps her arms around me and I fall into her squishy, comforting hug. I wait for the words I expect her to say, along the lines of, *How dare they? I've got a right mind to march around there and give them my what for! That is disgraceful!*

She says nothing, waiting instead to see if I have anymore words. I do, but I'm too exhausted, plus I'm sick of crying. I nibble on my toast, forcing it down as I need to keep up my strength to face this day, the first of which will be many hard days.

'You just tell me what you need from me,' Mum says.

'Thanks, Mum. I'm not really sure what I need. For now, I need another shower, a bit of lippy and to put my big girl pants on and go to work in my new community pantry.'

'That's a good idea, love, there's only one way forward, and that's forward.'

I pull out of the driveway and watch Mum wave to me from the front steps in my rearview mirror. I feel gratitude for this safe landing place.

I don't know how I'm going to get through this, but I have no choice. Life does not stop, even when you want it to.

24

SKYE

I can smell what we're having for dinner as soon as I turn into Mum's driveway with my window down. Some sort of curry, maybe the mince curry Mum makes that's packed with vegetables and is just as delicious served with mashed potato as it is spread on hot buttery toast. Comfort food. Bev's antidote for all ailments, including a broken heart.

'Hello, love, how was the pantry today?' Mum looks up from the pot she's stirring on the stove so I can kiss her on the cheek.

'It was busy. I had no idea so many people around town were struggling to get food on the table each week.' I grab a spoon and take a sample from the steaming pot.

'Yum, you're such a good cook. Maybe you could run a cooking class and teach a few others how to make the best mince curry in all of Australia.'

Bev laughs. 'It's not quite restaurant quality, but of course, I'd love to pass the recipe on.'

'What is the recipe?'

Bev taps the side of her head. 'It's all in here. A bit of this, a bit of that and a sprinkle of whatever you can find in the cupboard.'

I laugh. 'Another one of your secret recipes then.'

'Yes, passed down through the generations and ever evolving. You think mine is good, if only you'd been able to taste it when your grandmother made it.'

I start setting the table and Mum gestures to the pot of boiling potatoes.

'You make the best mash though, Skye. You're up.'

When we're sitting at the table with our steaming plates of comfort food and a glass of red wine in front of us, Mum goes silent.

'Candy came around today,' she says gently.

I put my splade of curry back onto my plate, instantly losing my appetite. The hurt starts in my chest and spreads over my whole body.

'I told her, she needs to leave you alone,' Mum continues, carefully watching as I start to shake.

'She does need to leave me alone. I never want to see her or Jackson again.' I thought I might be able to get through a whole day without crying but today is not that day.

'It will be okay, you will be okay,' Mum says, leaning over to hold my hands.

'I know. I know it will. But it doesn't feel okay. How could they? How dare they?'

If I direct all my anger towards Jackson and Candy, I can block out any niggling reminders that I have also committed this sin. I have been in Candy's position, I have done what Candy has done.

Bev sits quietly eating her dinner while I force a few mouthfuls down inbetween shaking sobs. I can't get through the whole meal and leave my wine untouched.

'I'm sorry Mum, I might have this later.'

'That's okay, love, that's okay.'

I gently push my chair out and go to clear my plate.

'Leave it, I'll pack up. You go and have your shower.'

I hiccup and sob myself to the bathroom and then the bedroom, wondering if people die from pain like this, because the last thing I feel like is living.

25

SKYE

T he light flicks on and I groan in protest. I haven't left my bedroom in days.

'Rightio Skye, time to get up.'

I sit up quickly at the sound of a familiar voice, the last person I expected to be standing in my bedroom. He's leaning on the door-frame, in faded blue jeans and a black shirt, looking dangerously hot. Not that I have anything romantic or sexy on my mind.

'Quinton? Am I dreaming?'

'No, this is not a dream. It's reality. And the reality is you need to get that butt out of bed, get dressed and come to work because the pigs are waiting.'

'That's right Skye Pie, you're up,' says a second male voice from behind Quinton.

I glare at Mum standing in the doorway. I don't mind Austin being here, he's like a brother, but being an absolute wreck, Quinton is the last person I want to see.

'What the fuck is going on? Why are you here?'

Mum walks in and starts getting clothes out of my drawers and cupboard.

'Quinton just happened to call to ask if you're available to do a few shifts, because he's got a whole lot of work to do after signing a new contract with Safeway, and not enough people to help. He needs someone with experience who can just step in. I told him you were a free agent and were not doing anything at the moment, so yes, you would love to come and help with the pigs.'

I lay back down and pull the covers over my head.

'Tell Quinton no, thank you, I would not like to come and help him with the pigs. I'm busy. Plus I have to go back to the pantry in a few days.'

'I'll cover your shifts at the pantry, and I'll get a few more volunteers.'

Someone pulls the covers back and I'm face to face with Quinton. 'The pigs are desperate, and they need you, and I need you, so get your butt out of that bed and get dressed. You're coming with me and Austin, whether you like it or not..'

Reluctantly, and blushing bright red, I tumble out of bed while Mum shoos the boys out of the room and starts throwing clothes into my overnight bag.

'What's with the suitcase, Mum?'

'I suggested to Quinton that you bunk up in the workers cottage, with Austin. He's staying out there at the moment while they've got so many projects on the go. I'm packing your suitcase for you.'

I protest but Quinton, still smouldering at my bedroom door, interrupts.

'Save your energy, Skye. It's going to be a busy week.'

With that, he leaves, his familiar scent lingering. I'm not sure if my knees are weak from this or the fact that I haven't eaten for a few days, since falling into a black hole over Jackson and Candy. It was Candy's visit that set me off. Even though I thought I was doing brilliantly when I got through my first couple of days at the pantry, there is obviously a limit to how long I could put on such a brave and happy face while my world was falling apart.

I sway slightly as the dark thoughts wash over me. The past few days I have felt paralysed, with no will to live. I am broken, snapped into a million tiny pieces, ready to be swept into the dust pan and thrown into the trash. Mum is watching closely and pulls me into a hug.

'It's going to be fine, Skye,' she says. 'One minute at a time, one hour at a time, and then eventually you'll be one day at a time. Get out there amongst those pigs that you have always loved. They will be the best cure for your broken heart.'

I am unable to speak. Mum hands me some underwear, a pair of long pants and a long-sleeved shirt.

'Straight to the shower for you. I don't think the pigs care, but you have to sit in the vehicle with Quinton and Austin for the whole drive to the farm, and they might care.'

Standing under the shower, my legs tremble, then my whole body trembles as I try and drown the vision I can't get out of my head of Candy and Jackson.

I bet Candy is having the time of her life now that I'm out of the way. She can stop sneaking around with her boyfriend and can tell every single person that sits in her hairdressing chair about how in love her and Jackson are, and how they're going to live *my* happily ever after.

I scrub away the shame of the betrayal which threatens to drown me.

Why should you feel ashamed?

I start my own personal pep talk.

You have nothing to be ashamed of. You didn't do anything wrong.

The hot water starts working a miracle on my attitude. The familiar smell of my strawberry shower soap refreshes me. I wash my wild, greasy hair, before spreading big blobs of cold conditioner on top of my head. I run my fingers through until my long locks are free of knots and let the smoothness comfort me.

As I wash my anger down the plug hole, I get a tiny glimpse and of my real self.

My thoughts take over again.

I hope Jackson has a scar from where I threw the giant engagement ring at his forehead.

Maybe the best thing is to get out of town for a whole week, away from the whispers and the gossips.

It looks like I'm not going to have to have the argument with Jackson about keeping my own surname.

It looks like I'm not going to have to have any arguments with him at all.

In fact, if I never lay eyes him ever again, my life will be a whole lot better.

After towel drying, I twist my hair into a long plait that falls down my back and squeeze the excess drips out the end. I hold on desperately to my small daily rituals. I smother myself in moisturiser and a generous spray of my favourite fruity perfume.

I catch Quinton's blush as I walk into the kitchen, before he quickly looks away. He admonishes himself, the last thing Skye will be thinking about is being with another man.

'I thought you might like something to eat, love, before you go.'

Mum is standing at the stove and the smell of frying bacon and eggs make my stomach growl loudly. We all laugh.

Austin hands me a glass of freshly-squeezed orange juice.

'It's from that tree in the back corner, it won't stop fruiting. The more Quinton picks, the more that grow.' Austin gestures to a box in the corner overflowing with fat, juicy, bright orange oranges.

'It's like that every year, and has been for as long as I remember,' I say, taking a long sip. 'So sweet, doesn't need a single thing added to it. Your Mum used to make all that marmalade, remember?'

'I do remember,' Austin says. 'I think there's probably still a few jars way up the back of the pantry. You'd better have a look Quinton, it will be like striking gold if you can find a jar.'

Quinton is standing beside Mum at the stove, expertly flipping the eggs to get them just like I like them, flipped on both sides and runny in the middle.

'Grab that toast would you Quinton, love,' she says, and Quinton butters the toast on the plates that Bev has arranged along the bench.

'Love?' I mimic, 'make yourself right at home.'

'Hey, love,' Quinton chuckles. 'Well, this is the third day Austin and I have been here for breakfast. I'm pretty familiar with the place.'

'The third day? Why have you been here every day?'

'To come and pick you up for work,' Austin says.

'I never knew you were here.'

'We're always here for you Skye,' Austin says, reaching out to pat me on the arm. 'We didn't realise what you had going on.'

'So the rumour mill didn't get out to the farm?'

'No, it didn't. Not much gets out to the farm,' Quinton chuckles and my knees weaken. I love that chuckle.

'On day one, Bev thought you'd had a pretty rough night, so she cooked us the best breakfast we've had in yonks, then we went off to work. We came back on day two with a slightly different purpose, as I wanted to check on how you were travelling. But again, it had been another rough night,' Austin continues.

Mum cuts in. 'And here we are, day three, and we just made the decision, no matter what sort of night you'd had, it was time to get you out of that bed.'

'Why do I feel ganged up on all of a sudden?'

Mum, Austin and Quinton exchange glances.

'We're not bossing you around,' Mum says. 'We're just here to help you get back on your feet.'

'I'm definitely not bossing you around,' Quinton says between mouthfuls, 'I'm not that silly. I just need someone to come and help with the pigs.'

I'm ravenous. I smile and resist the temptation to shovel my food in. 'It's nice to know I can still be useful.'

My voice quivers.

'I'm really sorry, Skye,' Quinton says. 'I can't imagine how sad you must feel.'

I push away the instinct to reassure him that I am okay, because as soon as I look into his eyes, I know he is someone I can be completely honest and frank around.

'Well, I am sad. But I'm also fucking furious!'

Quinton and Austin nearly choke on their eggs.

'That's my girl,' Bev says proudly. 'Now, eat your eggs and get your bum into gear. An angry woman gets a lot of shit done.'

Laughter fills the kitchen, and by the time I walk out the front door, I feel no hesitation or fear.

I breathe in the new day. *You've got this.*

...

I HARDLY RECOGNISE parts of the farm which has new sheds, new machinery, new roads, silos and concrete loading docks. Quinton is in his element amongst the hustle and bustle. Monty and Adeline are long gone, with their visas running out and having to return to France. Five new faces are working in the sheds, and a large number of pigs are free-ranging. I can see beautifully lush pastures in the distance with shiny fences.

I didn't tell Quinton in that conversation which feels like a lifetime ago, but I also studied permaculture after I left high school, and I've had my old notes out to reacquaint myself with the concepts of working with nature, growing nutritious food while looking after the environment and your own personal health and wellbeing. I've adopted those concepts in the community garden and tried to talk to Jackson about it after dinner one night, but he was less than interested.

He much preferred to talk about big machinery, big-time road contracts, big money, big this and big that.

After I've finished in the sheds for the day, I wander to a paddock that's been catching my eye all day. I couldn't make out from a distance what crop was growing in it, and the closer I get, I see that it's a mixture of different plants together.

The afternoon sun starts to take on its luminous glow, and unable to resist, I pull my boots and socks off and stand in amongst the plants, my toes wriggling down into the soil.

I feel someone come up behind me. Seeing my discarded boots and socks, Quinton follows suit.

'Never thought to take my shoes off at the end of the day like this,' he says.

'There's nothing like the feeling of fresh pasture and beautiful soil between your toes,' I reply. 'Not to mention a bit of squishy pig poo.'

'Haha, I didn't even notice. I think I've lost my sense of smell since coming here.'

'Same. I lost mine years ago!'

We laugh then ease into a comfortable silence as we watch the sky change colours.

'What is this paddock?' I ask.

'In America they call them cover crops. Basically they're plants used to protect and improve the soil when cash crops aren't being grown. Ideally, cover crops cover the soil for most or all of the year, providing living roots that soil microbes need in making the soils healthier.' He pauses. 'Too much info?'

'No, keep going. This is fascinating. I don't know of anyone who's doing anything like this on a large scale.'

'I cop a fair bit of ribbing at footy training and the pub. Everyone reckons I'm a hippie.'

'A hippie in a cowboy hat? Those are two types of people you don't see mixed together all that often.'

'Exactly. I might just be the first Australian cowboy hippie.'

'You might be. Regardless of any labels or name calling, this paddock looks incredible.'

'It does. I can't wait to see how it turns out in a few years.'

'Sounds like you're here to stay, cowboy.'

We stand in silence and the giant sky engulfs us as it turns from a golden wash to a deep orange.

'I might have some idea of how you're feeling,' he offers quietly.

A flash of anger finds its way from my toes to my mouth.

'Not likely. Do you know how it feels to walk in on your best friend and your fiancé naked in your bed, fucking their brains out?'

'Not quite,' Quinton replies, 'but broken hearted is broken hearted, true?'

'I guess.'

'It took me a while,' he continues, 'but I've found my feet now. After losing Beth, I lost myself and at the same time, I had to face up to what I had done to her. With you.'

I look shamefully at my bare toes in the dirt.

'I have been trying to block that out too,' I admit. I slowly raise my eyes to his. 'I never even thought what it might be like for Beth, to find out about us.'

Quinton's voice shakes. 'It was complicated. I thought she was having an affair with her ex, but as it turned out I had the wrong end of the stick. He was going through a life crisis, finally facing up to the fact he was gay, and she was there as a friend for him.'

'Oh, that is complicated.'

'Very much so. What that meant was I couldn't justify my actions as payback. I was just a straight out lying, cheating boyfriend. Not much different to a lying, cheating fiancé.'

I take in big gulps of air as the sky continues its bright, brilliant sunset theatre show. I feel small and insignificant under such a big sky.

I feel tears prick like tiny pins in my eyes.

Quinton kneels down to pull out a plant and proudly shows me the roots.

'Have you ever seen roots like this?'

I laugh. Talk about gear change. 'Only in the community garden.'

'Of course, sorry, I forgot I'm talking to an expert.' Quinton blushes.

'Nah, I'm just teasing you. And I'm no expert.'

'The cover crops are like a Swiss Army knife with a few different tools for things like soil health, soil erosion, weed control, managing nutrients, and better water quality.' Quinton is on a roll, and I laugh.

'You have a new obsession, don't you.'

'True. I do.'

The sun is dipping lower and it won't be long before dark. I move towards my socks and boots and roughly dust the soil off, balancing on one leg to put each sock on. Quinton does the same and we fall sideways into each other.

'What do I look like,' I laugh, 'A PLP?'

'You are making me feel my age. What's a PLP?'

'Sorry old fella, public leaning post.'

Quinton laughs. 'I might steal that one.'

'Sure, you can have it.'

In companionable silence we stride up the hill as the sky bursts into its final glorious moment of the day, in a kaleidoscope of orange, yellow, deep pink and purple.

'I have a few regrets,' Quinton says, out of the blue. 'One that I let you leave here, just to cover my own selfish arse.'

I don't break my stride, feeling lighter than I have for weeks. 'That's ancient history, Quinton. Honestly, don't sweat it. As it turns out, my work life is great. It's forced me out of my routine and made me look over the fence a bit more.'

Quinton is silent until we reach the front gate of the homestead, which is directly opposite to the front gate of the cottage where I'm bunked up with Austin.

'I really want you to come back and work here, permanently. You've got so many skills and so much experience. I could use having someone as a sounding board with all this soil and permaculture stuff. Austin told me you've done a permaculture course, you never mentioned it.'

'Austin told me you're a Nuffield Scholar, you never mentioned that.'

'So we're even.'

'Pretty much.'

I go to leave and Quinton reaches out to touch my arm. 'I mean it, I'm offering you a job, but not the same job you had before. More of an on-farm management role. I'm going to be away a lot and need someone here I can trust.'

'What about Austin?'

'Austin's leaving. He first said he was going to stay for a few months after we bought it, that turned into a year and I've lost count of how long he's been here now. He wants to go on an overseas ag exchange and learn a bit more about the world. He doesn't have a set plan and might end up back here, or might not.'

'That's exciting for him. Bloody bugger never said a thing.'

'He's playing his cards close to his chest, as per usual. People round here too, they think it's a crock of shit. He hasn't told anyone he got a scholarship to look into this thing in the US that they call regenerative agriculture. Kind of what we're trying out here, changing the mix of conventionally grown pastures, cutting back on the chemicals and looking at everything we do on the farm to see how we can add-value. The neighbours reckon we've gone nutty.'

'Who cares what people say. If we spent our lives worrying about what people think and say, we'll never be able to move forwards. I can't wait to pick Austin's brain, that sounds amazing.'

'Yeah, I'd love to do something like that. One day, but I need to pay down a bit of this debt first. Get things profitable and make sure I can deliver what the supermarket contract dictates.'

It's almost dark and I can't see Austin's features, just the outline of his hat and profile.

'I'd better get into the shower and ready for bed, today wiped me out,' I say, reluctant to leave but feeling dead on my feet.

'About the job offer, I'll think about it. I don't know whether I'm in the best place to be making any life-altering decisions.'

'There's no rush,' Quinton says quickly, 'The offer's there. Take your time.'

'Thanks. And thanks for getting me out of my own misery. It's what I needed to pull me out of my slump.'

In the darkness I can hide the pain in my eyes.

'I always find if you can get yourself out of bed every day and just take a few steps, it's a whole lot better than lying around feeling sorry for yourself and ending up in a constant spiral. I've never really been one to staying in bed, but there have been days where it's been pretty hard to walk out the door.'

'It happens to me every once in a while, I just can't seem to lift out of it,' I say.

'I know exactly what you need,' Quinton says, and I can hear it in his voice that he's got a cheeky grin. 'What you need is a whole lot of four-legged friends relying on you to look after them, so every day you *have* to get up. You've got no choice.'

I burst out laughing, the first laugh in a long time.

'True, that's very true. We can't let those pigs down, those precious, precious pigs.'

'The pig whisperer, that's what you are.' Quinton says so quietly that I don't hear him.

At that moment the lights of the cottage come on and Austin comes cluttering down the front steps.

'There you are! I've just put the barbie on – anyone fancy some dinner?'

'I hope you're not cooking pork.' I laugh.

'Nah. Steak. What do you reckon Quinton? Time to get a few cows?'

'No way, we've got enough going on here!' Quinton opens his gate and heads towards the house. 'See youse later, I've got bookwork to do.'

'Oh my gosh, pigs and cows. That is perfect, you need to convince Quinton to get some cows,' I say to Austin as I wander into the cottage. 'I love cows.'

'I heard that,' Quinton yells out. 'And the answer is no!'

...

THE FOLLOWING MORNING, at dawn, I find myself back in the cover crop to watch the sunrise. I've had the first peaceful sleep I've had since, well, you know when, and wonder if I should seriously consider Quinton's offer. It is so tranquil out here, away from prying eyes. I could spend my days with pigs and in the paddocks, a much more attractive option to avoiding people on the street who are whispering behind their hands and having a field day with the multitude of versions of the story of *Skandy and Jackson*.

I watch the sun slowly appear over the mountains that surround the farm, giving a golden hue to the swaying grasses across the paddock.

With a light, cool breeze fanning my cheeks, I'm back where I belong, in nature, with my bare feet in the dirt. I don't know how things will turn out, but does it matter?

I'm just a tiny speck in a giant landscape. This moment shall pass, as will the next, and the next. Life will carry me along regardless. It's my choice entirely if I ride under a black cloud or let the light in.

26

SKYE

Time has marched on, as it does, and the unexpected explosion of my engagement, wedding plans and happily ever after dreams is getting further behind me.

I've completely changed my life by resigning from my public-facing job at the RSL Club and shifting back out to Quinton's farm to live in the cottage and manage the pigs.

I still work every now and then at the nursery when Mrs Mac needs a break, and I have my two days at the community pantry with Mum. She's taken it on as a full-time passion and I am keeping Quinton's garden going, and we never run short on fresh fruit and vegetables.

I no longer need to run to my secret spot by Dart Brook Creek and cry. I still worry about the garden I so lovingly brought to life but most days I feel relieved I didn't marry Jackson and that he's no longer part of my world. I can see more clearly that I was marrying an idea, a concept, a childhood fantasy. The perfect house with the perfect husband. Jackson has proven there is no such thing.

I'm training extra hard and cram every minute of every day with something to stop my mind from going into deep, dark places where the vision of Candy sitting on Jackson's face lurks. The rabbit holes that take me into spiralling thoughts of when, where, why and how are gradually closing over.

Quinton and I? There is no Quinton and I.

Sure, the attraction is there but I feel dead inside. It's not the time to be picking up my cowboy obsession and making him into something he isn't or using him to make me feel better. He's away a lot and that's put extra responsibilities on my shoulders, especially with Austin also gone.

Today I am at the nursery while Mrs Mac has a meeting in Sydney with a wedding venue owner who saw the brochures I made of her flower arrangements. Once word gets around, she will need to put on extra staff to keep up with the wedding orders.

I relish in being surrounded by plants and flowers and don't have a single second of thinking time thanks to the steady stream of customers. I end up working well after closing time after a spark of late-afternoon inspiration resulted in losing myself for hours rearranging the window display. My mix of lush and desert plants in terracotta pots of all shapes and sizes will have indoor plant lovers streaming through the door.

The late afternoon sun is blindingly bright as I walk to the car just on sunset and I don't see him at first, casually leaning against the driver's door, arms folded.

He's dressed in tradie clothes – a fluorescent yellow shirt and navy shorts, steel capped boots and a navy cap with his business logo, *Groundbreakers*. He is staring intently, a look of remorse and regret across his face.

My spine stiffens, and I keep my face stonily blank as I walk towards the car.

'I'm not interested in talking to you,' I say curtly as I attempt to push past. He refuses to move.

'Please, please Skye. I've tried every way I know how to talk to you, you've sent back all my letters, unopened. I'm not going to give up until you explain, you can't avoid me forever,' he says, his dark brooding eyes drilling into mine.

'Explain what? Explain how you and my best friend have been

fucking the whole time we were engaged, actually even before we were engaged.'

'It's not like what you think,' he pleads, standing up tall and towering over me. He reaches out to hold my hands. I try and slap him away, his touch like a red-hot fire poker.

'It's you that I love, Skye. It's you that I want,' he says softly, his deep voice thick with regret.

'Give me a break. That's the biggest crock of shit I have ever heard in my life,' I spit, unable to control myself. 'You obviously weren't thinking about me while you with Candy, sneaking around behind my back, doing the most awful thing you can do to someone who loves you.' Tears threaten as my words spew out, and I will myself to hold it together.

'I'm sorry, I have no excuse for the way I treated you. I was so caught up in myself, my big plans and my own importance. I was careless, thoughtless, thinking I was bulletproof. I don't know how it happened or why I did it. But it's not Candy I want, it's you. It's always been you.'

He is still holding my hands, and I start to shake. Every sense in my body wants to disappear into his familiar arms and let all the built-up tension go. It's the first time I've laid eyes on him since that day, although it's not for his lack of trying. For a while Candy tried diligently to see me too, but Bev wouldn't let her near me. Living in a small town, it's miraculous we haven't crossed paths, but I have been keeping my movements small to minimise the risk. The latest is that she's left Scone, so I no longer need to worry about running into her in the dairy section or the pasta aisle in the supermarket.

He gently lifts my chin so I am looking up at him, moving closer at the same time. I notice a tiny scar in the middle of his forehead and shake even harder.

'Skye, please. I've changed, I truly have. I've been going to counselling...'

'Counselling?' I whisper. 'You?'

'Mum made me.'

'Your Mum?'

'Yeah, she doesn't want to see my future turn out the way...' Jackson's voice trails off.

'...the way your Dad's has,' I finish for him, gently. Everyone knows how much his Dad flirts around town, but I have never indulged in the rumours as I know how out of proportion things get in a small community each time a story is repeated in the hairdressing salon, the pub or the footy clubrooms.

'How can she stay? I don't understand,' I mumble, my words slicing into my own heart.

'She left, a long time ago. They've been fairly private about it all.' Jackson has tears in his eyes and I feel a tiny chink in my fury armour.

'You have first-hand experience of what a mess it makes when you do this to the person you're supposed to be committed to, and you still kept seeing Candy behind my back?' I'm crying openly.

Jackson pulls me into his chest and wraps his arms around me. At first I resist but he holds me tight and I end up collapsing into him, breathing in his familiar smell, my head fitting just left of centre in that place where his biceps are the perfect shape to snuggle into. More than a full head taller than me, he gently kisses the top of my head, repeating softly.

'I'm sorry, I'm sorry, I'm sorry. I didn't mean to hurt you so bad. There's nothing between me and Candy anymore, not now, not ever.'

I want to stay here forever. It's not until this moment I realise how much I have missed him and the life we were planning. He is my first grown-up love, my first real lover, my first of so many things. We have shared my most intimate of sexual experiences. I've grown up with him, in my bed, in my heart. My tears soak into his fluorescent shirt as the light fades into darkness.

Eventually we pull apart. I'm sniffling and he reaches into his pocket and hands me his hanky.

'Is it clean?' I ask, like I always do. He chuckles, that familiar, throaty chuckle that gets me every time.

'Clean enough,' is his standard reply. Followed by, 'but it's not now' as I blow into it.

We lean side by side against the car, our shoulders touching. Time stands still.

Jackson moves to stand in front of me again. 'Can you please, please come home, Skye. I can't live without you,' he says, his nose touching mine, his eyes glistening with emotion. 'And neither can the garden!' There's that chuckle again.

I don't move, my mind and heart having an internal battle where neither is giving in.

He cups my face in his hands.

'Forgive me,' he whispers hoarsely. 'Forgive me, please.'

I stare into his eyes for the longest time.

Can I forgive him?

27

QUINTON

I watch her headlights as she drives at her usual Nanna-driver speed towards the main gate. I'm in the front sunroom which I've converted to an office because I love its all the way round glass windows that give me a west, south-west view. I can also see who's coming and going as they drive up the hill past the piggery before they arrive at the homestead.

I've tried to keep my distance since Skye moved out here to manage the farm, but it's not easy living less than five hundred metres away from the woman I fall more in love with every day. We have unfinished business, I know it, but she has lost the sparkle in her eyes. I don't want to be anyone's rebound. Not after what I went through with Beth, who I genuinely believed was *the one*. When she left, I rebounded, multiple times. I'm not proud of my drunken one-night stands, and know I hurt people. I want Skye, desperately, but I don't want to mess it up, or mess her up.

I wander out to the kitchen. There's one spot where I have a clear view of Skye's gate and front door, and wonder if she'll pop in and say hello. She doesn't. I watch her load herself up so she is carrying six bags in each hand, one trip only. She uses a thumb to lift the latch and pushes open the gate with her foot, and struggles up the steps as the bags get heavier. She dumps them on the mat which says *Welcome Home* and unlocks the door. I hear the now-familiar rattle of the timber sign she's hung on the door which is painted with pink piglets and flowers and reads *Home Sweet Home*.

She takes one lot of bags inside and her verandah light comes on, illuminating her like a rock star under the spotlight. Feeling like a stalker, I turn back towards the office but just as I do, I notice when she comes back for her next load of bags her shoulders are shaking and she's wiping her eyes. Is she crying? What should I do?

I don't even hesitate, and take giant strides towards the door, grab my hat from the hook and put it on out of habit, pull my boots on, slide open and take the steps two at a time.

She doesn't hear me, but as soon as I'm outside I can hear her sobbing. I want to run but it's not in my nature.

'Hey Skye,' I call out.

She's under her verandah light, giving me a clear view of her red eyes and trembling shoulders.

'You right? Need help?'

'I'm fine. Thanks. I don't need any help.' She definitely needs help.

I push her gate open, breathing in the intoxicating scent of sweet peas that are flowering the full length of the front fence, and walk slowly up the steps. She doesn't move but the closer I get the more her shoulders shake.

'You're not fine,' I say as I wrap my arms around her. She cries into my chest and I hug her tightly. She pushes me away.

'I'm sorry, I really am fine, I'll be fine,' she says between sniffs and sobs.

'What's happened? Is it your Mum?'

'No, not Mum.' She wipes her eyes and takes a deep breath.

'You can tell me.'

She stops crying, wipes her eyes one final time and tucks her hair behind her ears.

'I don't want to talk about it.'

'You can talk to me. You know you can.'

I raise one eyebrow. I'm not going anywhere. Minutes pass in silence, me looking at her, her looking at me, and she gradually comes down off that ledge.

'Jackson came to see me, after work. It's the first time I've spoken to him.'

'The first time in all this time?'

'Yes. I've got my own personal security guard, Bev, and here, my hideaway. I haven't answered any of his calls, or opened any of his letters.'

'I had no idea you've been bottling all this up for all this time, no wonder you're a wreck.' Skye sticks her chin out defensively.

'I'm not a wreck, I'm perfectly together.'

I raise my one eyebrow again.

'What did he say?'

Skye chokes up and her eyes go glassy.

'He asked me to come back, begged me actually. He pleaded, apologised and asked for forgiveness.'

I hold my breath, not sure how to react. Part of me feels fury for what Jackson and Candy have done, the other part of me knows I can't judge. Even though Beth and I weren't in a good place, I didn't exactly display model behaviour with Skye.

'And?' I ask softly.

'When I was in his arms, it felt like I *could* forgive him. I wanted to go back, to my home, the home that I loved, the man that I loved, the life that I loved, the garden that I loved.'

She starts shaking again and I long to hold her, but I don't. Silent tears roll down her cheeks and she wrings her hands as she speaks.

'I told him I would follow him home, and for a few blocks I did. But when I got to the end of the street I realised I can never go back into that house, I can never sleep in that bed again, I can't prepare dinner in that kitchen. There's pain in every room.'

Still crying quietly, she looks up at me with her dark brown, almost black eyes fringed by her long lashes stuck together by tears.

'I turned around and drove here. Where it's safe. Where I'm safe.'

I reach out with my cold hand and touch her hot cheek. She puts her hand over mine and holds it there.

'You're hot,' I say. She smiles weakly. 'I didn't mean that kind of hot, I just mean your cheek is hot, you are hot, temperature hot.' She grins and like a contagious yawn, I find myself also grinning.

'You're hotter,' she says, and I see it. That sparkle.

I take my hat off and place it gently on the arm of the old three-seater lounge that she's covered with a blue and white check blanket and bright yellow cushions, her favourite reading place. She hasn't moved. I take my time and walk slowly to her, every nerve on fire.

We stand as close as we can without touching. My breathing quickens and I wonder if her heart is racing as fast as mine. Without breaking eye contact I lean in. Her eyes widen as I move closer. The branch snaps as my lips graze hers and we lose control, grabbing wildly at each other's clothes without breaking lip contact, kissing deeper, tongues probing, hands exploring. Our breathing gets louder and within minutes we are both naked, standing under the brightness of her verandah light, our bodies wrapped around each other as though she wants to get inside my skin and me inside hers.

Unable to control ourselves we stumble onto the couch. We break lips, briefly, as she swipes away the cushions, then we rejoin as she pulls me on top of her. My hands want to be everywhere at once and they move through her hair, to her face, down her arms. She moans and arches her back as I move off her lips and down her neck to lick her fully erect nipples, trying to fit as much of her into my mouth as I can. She moves my hands down her stomach and to her swollen lips, which are slick and ready. I feel myself harden against her thigh and move back to her mouth to kiss her. She grabs my arse cheeks and moves me over her, moaning into my mouth, and I know exactly what she wants because I want it too.

I'm about to lose my mind and want to be inside her more desperately than I've ever wanted to be inside someone, but pull away in a moment of panic. 'I don't have a condom.'

'It's okay, you don't need one,' she groans. 'We have unfinished business and I need to feel you, all of you, every bit of you, inside me, *now*.'

I notch my head against her entrance and hear her groan in pleasure. She feels mind-blowingly tight and I slide gently across her wetness, wanting to savour the moment as much as wanting to be inside her. 'So tight,' I groan as I push in further, feeling more sensation than I ever imagined. The deeper and harder I go the louder she calls my name. 'Quinton, Quinton, Quinton. More, give me more, harder, faster,' she calls. No longer able to hold back, I pound into her and the couch moves across the verandah.

I don't know if I can wait but I don't want it to be over for her so soon.

'I want you to come for me, babe.'

Her eyes widen and she moans.

'Call me babe and I'm already there,' she moans.

'Babe.'

'I'm coming, I'm coming, harder, Quinton, there, there!' I hold myself back and watch her eyes go wide as she grips me with her orgasm. I stop, briefly, before I pull myself out, then back in, slowly at first, then faster.

'More?' I ask, watching her face closely.

In reply, she grips both of my arse cheeks and pulls me deeper into her. I don't take my eyes off hers as I take her to the brink again.

'Give it to me, more, *now*!' she orders, and I obey.

'You're so beautiful,' I whisper as I watch her orgasm a second time. I almost lose control, almost. I want to give her even more, so I slow myself down and move slowly out, then back in, out, then in. 'Can you take more?'

She pushes me out and flips me onto my back. 'Can you take more?' she asks as she moves my hands onto her tits. I watch her lower herself onto me, and she arches her back as I slide deeper inside her wetness.

'Oh, you're wet,' I sigh, twisting and flicking her nipples until they're rock hard. She moves up and down on my cock, swirling her hips in one direction, then the other, staring into my eyes. She runs her hands over my chest as she makes me pound into her and every nerve ending in my body is alight. She moves faster and I close my eyes, feeling sensations I've never felt before.

'Skye, I want it, I want you so bad,' I moan.

'Take it, take me, take me all, I'm yours, I'm all yours. It's time to finish what you started,' she screams as she moves up and down on my slick cock. I lose all control, surging, twitching and throbbing at the same time she grips and trembles. We call out in unison. 'There, there!'

With me still inside her, she collapses onto me as we say at the same time.

Jinx on the there there.

Jinx on the there there.

We laugh, both fully spent, and she lays her hot, naked body over mine like an electric blanket turned on three. I feel her heart beating through my chest as I gently pull out. Our bodies slick with sweat and cum, she kisses my chin and I kiss her forehead, running my fingers softly through her long, tangled hair.

'There,' I whisper, overwhelmed with emotion.

'There,' she whispers back.

Eventually she rolls off and pulls on my shirt. I lift my legs so she can sit on the couch, and she pulls them over her lap.

'You look good in my shirt,' I say.

'That's original.'

'It is original,' I protest.

'Mmmm, I think you might have heard that in a song. Keith Urban's the cowboy that came up with that line.'

'He stole it from me.'

'I'm sure he did. That's got cowboy written all over it.'

'It does, 'cause I'm a cowboy.'

'Yes, you are. A *real* cowboy. My dream cowboy. The cowboy I want, need and have just had.'

KEEP IN TOUCH WITH MISSY B

Email Missy at missybestwrites@gmail.com

Search for *Missy Best Writes Spice* on TikTok, Instagram and Facebook